All Jingled Out

Two Sweet-and-Light
Tales of "Mom Ingenuity"
in the Wake of
Holiday Mayhem

PAMELA DOWD
CHRISTINE LYNXWILER

BARBOUR
PUBLISHING

Published by Barbour Publishing, Inc., P.O. Box 719, Uhrichsville, Ohio 44683, www.barbourbooks.com

Our mission is to publish and distribute inspirational products offering exceptional value and biblical encouragement to the masses.

 Member of the
Evangelical Christian
Publishers Association

Printed in the United States of America.
5 4 3 2 1

All Jingled Out

All Done with the Dashing

by Pamela Dowd

Dedication

My Lord Jesus: I count it all joy to have Your encouragement as I walk this narrow writing path.

I'm not Maggie, nor is my family hers, but we can relate. To Rodney, my husband of a million miles, and to Abigail, Lindsay, Natalie, and Wade: You pray, believe, and encourage my stories into print.

To my critique group: Jeanne, Vickie, Ruth, Nancy, Shelley, and Paula. You keep me inspired. Smile when you read your suggestions in print.

To Deidre Knight, my agent: You help me believe I can write all things through Christ.

To Charles and Gloria Fletcher: Thanks for genetic creativity and generous applause.

To Shannon Hill, my editor: You have refreshed my heart.

To Susan Downs, my copy editor: Your suggestions were like cream added to smooth coffee.

Chapter 1

Maggie Mackenzie's slippers crunched into the predawn snow as she lifted the latch and pushed open the neighbor's gate. She felt vulnerable dressed in her bathrobe with flashlight in hand at 3:00 a.m. *How ironic! I look like a "cat" burglar.* She snickered, and her mouth curved into a smile. Her breath formed little puffs in the morning air. It was unusually cold for east Texas.

Who's insane enough to be slogging around in the middle of the night taking care of a furry little chore on her to-do list? She rolled her eyes. *I am.*

Maggie's every step shattered the layer of crust on the fragile, frosted ground. Icy crumbs lodged between her socks and fuzzy house shoes. She shivered.

She worked her way along the bushes to her neighbor's garage and felt for the hidden key above the door.

Her fumbling, cold fingers bumped the key, and she listened as it glanced off the concrete into what sounded like leaves. *Great!*

She tightened the belt on her plaid flannel robe and dropped to her knees. She shined the light and felt along the wall, her fingers growing numb. She cringed at the thought of searching the sticky, damp leaf pile blown into the corner by the rainstorm before the snow. Maggie had a good mind to march home, sleep late, and tell her family there'd be no Thanksgiving dinner this year.

She could send the family to McDonald's. . .and ship Samson, the cat expecting breakfast, to join his owners on their cruise. No plunging her hand into Thanksgiving Tom with his innards wadded in paper. No stinky giblet gravy for lunch.

Had her husband, David, ever noticed no one else liked that kind of gravy? *I've pointed it out often enough. I can hear him now: "But, honey. It wouldn't be the holidays without giblets."* It wouldn't be the "holidays" without the stuff everybody else expected *her* to do.

Maggie hoped the twenty-pound bird back at the house had cooperated in the thawing process and wasn't as frozen as her tender feet. It'd be her luck, although she'd defrosted it according to the package directions.

On her second stab into the pile, her fingers seized

the cold metal key. She fumbled with the lock and entered the darkened garage, her nose instantly assaulted by the disgusting odors of gas and motor oil.

"Here, kitty! Samson? You in here? I have breakfast. . .or a late midnight snack. . .whatever. I have food."

Metal pelted the concrete, startling Maggie. She yelped, spinning toward the clatter. Her light revealed the mystery—a toppled tin of scattered nails.

Samson stretched and mewed while she recovered. He rubbed against her pajamas.

Maggie placed the cat food on the hood of the Suburban. As the opener circled the can, she tried not to scratch the paint. Pervasive canned liver quickly overcame all garage smells, and Samson jumped to attention beside her. She scratched his ear. "Watch your tongue on that sharp can," she warned as she left.

Picking her way home, she looked at the stars. *Well, Lord, here we are. Just the two of us. Another Thanksgiving. Another time to be thankful. Sorry, God, I hadn't noticed.* She checked her watch by the moonlight. *Off schedule already!*

Hadn't God set her up in this crazy life? A proverb came to mind. *"She looketh well to the ways of her household." And her neighbors' household, and her in-laws, and the cat's meals.* Maggie tapped the flickering flashlight and chuckled. " 'Her candle goeth not out by night,' " she whispered.

She hoped God understood all she had on her plate. Make that *platter.*

She tiptoed back into the house, careful not to disturb the cousins littering the den floor that adjoined her kitchen. Cooking by candlelight wasn't romantic. *Stupid is more like it, but it's a sacrifice I'll gladly make to keep them all sleeping and "relatively" happy.* Preparing turkey in the dark was likely to result in a missing giblet or two, but if they came out in the dressing, she'd claim she meant to do it, and David would be pleased.

Contemplating the turkey in the sink, she placed one arm across her middle. The robe was still cold from her trek. *I need coffee. Bad.* She'd wanted to avoid waking the family with the aroma but decided to forget it. Who would wake at this hour of night?

"Morning," she whispered, correcting her internal monitor. *It's morning, and I have a turkey to dress and bake. Why have I wasted all this time on a stupid cat when I have a houseful of people expecting a meal it will take me hours to prepare and them minutes to eat?*

Maggie inhaled the cold thought. She hadn't considered how desperate she felt until she held the butcher knife over the turkey, ready to clip the plastic cord holding its wings. Standing alone in the candlelit kitchen, knife in hand. . .snoring relatives sprawled on the floor. Well, there was no telling what she might do—with the bird.

Chapter 2

Worn out, yet pleased with her sacrifice, Maggie looked at Thanksgiving Tom. He brought fresh meaning to "dressed for success." While the household slept, Maggie crept back to bed, savoring the mingled aromas of coffee and cinnamon. Her Twizzler-shaped pumpkin dough could rise undercover while she slept.

She situated her cold, socked feet along David's shins. His soft snoring ceased, then resumed when she grew still. As she collapsed into a deep sleep, no visions of holi-daze danced in *her* head.

In the way known only to sleeping mothers, Maggie sensed her three-year-old standing at her elbow. She cast a selfish prayer heavenward—*Lord, send him back*

to sleep—before peeking to see if it'd worked. It hadn't.

Brophy nudged her arm. Then he patted her cheek.

Maggie rolled toward David, feigning sleep. David hadn't awakened and probably wouldn't.

Maybe ignoring him would send Brophy scurrying. Surely, he wouldn't find a sleeping mommy half as endearing as she found a sleeping boy. *I only need forty thousand more winks.* She remained still.

Brophy stroked her hair. "It's Pilgrim and Indian day, Mama," he said in his wake-up voice. "And somebody's been in the kitchen."

This wasn't news to Maggie. She'd already experienced a turkey baster full of fun. Maggie hoped her dreary attitude wasn't contagious. For fear of harming her offspring, she harrumphed without a sound. *Pilgrim and Indian Day! I'd like to scare up some pilgrims to help cook my feast.*

"I want break-a-fust. Come on." Brophy climbed onto the bed and tugged her shoulder.

Maggie rolled toward the boy perched on his knees. Behind one hand, she perfected a yawn.

Brophy reached down for a hug, then lunged for Maggie in giggles. He squeezed her cheeks between chubby little fists and laughed at her fish lips.

Maggie drank in his dimpled smile, his sleep-tousled hair; he looked so glad to see her. How could she resist such. . . Her eyelids grew heavy before she could finish the thought.

Brophy's tickling fingers reminded Maggie she was supposed to be awake. Brophy smelled like the dog he slept with. Maggie didn't know why she bothered to bathe him at night except to give Scruffy a clean boy to lick.

Brophy pried one of Maggie's eyes open with his icy little fingers. "Mama, wake up."

Maggie pulled away, shaking her head side to side. "Stop. What do you want?" She didn't mean to sound grouchy. She popped her eyes open before Brophy could and looked at his expectant face. Maggie heaved a sigh.

She threw back the comforter and edged her legs off the bed while Brophy jumped to the floor. "Okay, son. Let me get my bearings." She clutched the nightstand. "Is the room spinning, or is it just my imagination? Give me a second. I have to find my robe."

Brophy darted to the bathroom, grabbed it off the linoleum, and returned.

"Why don't you ever wake your daddy?"

" 'Cause all Daddy gives me is Loops from the bottom shelf."

"Where you can reach them," she interjected.

"I want pannercakes." He took her hand and squeezed it tight.

She walked toward the kitchen, swinging his hand

along in hers. "Not this morning, sweetie. Mommy's way too tired to remember how to make them."

What she saw jolted her as much as if she'd thrown the car into reverse expecting to go forward. Instantly awake, her eyes followed the floury cat tracks circling her navy tile floor. She gasped at the sight of paw prints marring her perfect rolls. Samson gazed at her with hooded lids, then returned to licking his paw. "This morning's breakfast might be your last supper!" She grabbed the cat under the belly and headed to the door where she dumped him into the cold. She turned on her son. "How'd he get in? Brophy, do you know anything about this?"

"The kitty was crying." Brophy had the pot drawer open.

"Don't you ever let that cat back in this house. You hear me?" Her voice conveyed the seriousness of his offense, but he looked so cute she almost laughed.

He dragged the big iron griddle across the floor, scraping the tile without repentance. She rescued the floor and sighed. "Go wake the family." *Maybe I'll get some help that way.* Maggie glanced at the kitchen clock. She'd slept only two hours. *There's got to be a better way than dashing through the snow.*

She heard her own miniature Paul Revere announce breakfast, "Come on, everybody! Pannercakes are coming."

15

Maggie dead-bolted the back door and hid the key. After cleaning Samson's mess, she selected four eggs, ticking off the number needed for the afternoon meal. *Two for each pumpkin and sweet potato pie.* She cracked an egg into the bowl. *Two—or was it four—for the pecan?* Another eggshell split with precision. *The gingerbread men for the non-pie eaters will take two. Thank goodness I bought two dozen.*

Maggie dipped into the Bisquick box and offered up a sigh of thanks for convenience foods about the time Brophy shuffled in with his Spiderman undies and pajamas down around his ankles. Maggie stared without compassion.

"Brophy, after Christmas, bud, we're tackling this problem. Your days of being catered to are over." Maggie blew the hair from her forehead and turned down the griddle.

The cousins laughed as Brophy waddled by.

Brophy puckered his bottom lip and stuck out his tongue.

"You see?" Maggie said to him. "You're too big for this. They won't even take you into Parents' Day Out until you learn to wipe yourself. You want to go to Parents' Day Out, don't you?" It was a conversation they oft repeated, but the adventure had not called Brophy's name, nor had he signed on the pottied line.

At the bathroom door, Maggie lost it. "How could one little boy make this big a mess?"

She surveyed the damage to her guest bathroom. The Golden Book, once perched on Brophy's lap, had fallen by the tub. A brown trail ran across the seat where he'd scooted to stand, and the toilet paper he'd tried to use littered the floor in stained wads. "Brophy Mackenzie!"

David came to the door.

"He's yours." Maggie walked passed him. "I splurged on Clorox wipes. They're under the sink."

David called after her, "It's about time you trained him."

Maggie stuffed a frustrated comeback aimed at the man bearing the initials H.U.S.B.A.N.D. She didn't have time to defend herself.

Chapter 3

Maggie stared at her brimming Thanksgiving plate and wondered if she would fall face-forward into the mashed potatoes, or if she'd still be awake when it came time to top the desserts with the fresh cream she'd whipped to perfection. She didn't have enough strength to lift the utensil in her hand, and she wasn't hungry.

Maggie twirled the fork though the green bean casserole and used it to slice a trench between several pecans atop the buttery warm sweet potato mountain next to her homemade cranberry sauce. She stabbed a mandarin orange—the ambrosia was about the only food she hadn't sampled—but she couldn't bring it to her mouth. Nothing looked tasty.

"Maggie, this is delicious. I don't know how you do it every year," her cousin said, lifting a forkful of green beans.

I don't either. Maggie gave a weak nod of thanks.

She knew the script. Next her father-in-law, Pop Mackenzie, would mention the close proximity of this holiday to Christmas and its do-again menu.

Pop didn't disappoint. He patted Maggie's hand and, like a coach wanting to inspire his best player, said, "Can hardly believe we get to do this all over again in four weeks."

She could have predicted the table conversation almost word for word. After a round of compliments, the football talk began. Maggie thought she might burst from the room with her ears covered. *Same. Same. Same. Always the same conversation.* She didn't care who carried the ball on the third down of the Cowboys game against the Dolphins in 1993, nor did she care who would play the Cowboys today—as un-Texan as that seemed. And she didn't want any more compliments.

Her quietness must have been misinterpreted, because her new sister-in-law, Charlie's wife, Jill, said, "Don't be so bashful. You could give us all cooking lessons. I know I'd sign up."

Charlie punched Jill in jest. "She needs some. I never knew water could burn until I married her."

"That was his fault." She addressed those listening.

He sent an inflated wink to his honeymoon cutie, causing her cheeks to splotch. "You're the one who lured me into the bedroom."

Maggie covered Brophy's ears for fear Charlie would elaborate.

Charlie received a swift kick under the table. David's brother needed someone to restrain him; it was nice to see he'd found a well-suited wife for the task.

Charlie held his shin with an exaggerated pout, a male-dominant Mackenzie trait.

Brophy imitated him.

Maggie rolled her eyes at Charlie. "Oh, sure, indoctrinate him early," she said, indicating Brophy with a nod as she cut a small bite of turkey and pushed it around in the gravy on her plate.

"What are you talking about?" Pop turned a bent lip south.

"That, that. . .that. . .that. . . ," Ma Mackenzie stammered, pointing at Pop's mouth.

"Frown," Maggie supplied the word Ma's dementia had stolen.

Ma grew serious. "I was going to say elephant." Her eyebrows pinched together as she considered her blunder.

Brophy whispered to Maggie while everyone could hear, "Did Ma get her words mixed up again?"

Maggie leaned close to his ear. "Shh. Eat your mac and cheese."

Brophy demonstrated the Mackenzie pout to perfection.

Maggie's sister, Anne, said, "As usual, Mags, you outdid yourself." She leaned back. "Do you know how much I look forward to this meal every year? And. . ." She looked around the table and included everybody in a self-tanned smile. ". . .to coming home?"

"Twice," Maggie said under breath.

"Excuse me?" Her sister missed the point.

"Twice. I cook this meal *twice* a year. And you come home twice." *And watch football. Twice. And compliment me. Twice. And fail to help. Twice.*

Anne looked for support. "Pop's already pointed that out. Haven't you, Pop?"

"Here. Here." David tapped on his glass of sparkling cider. The spoon-to-crystal sound drew everyone's attention. "I don't know how we'd manage without Maggie. Three cheers for Mags." He led the family in hip-hip-hoorays.

The eating began again after the prayer that someone remembered "because God deserved a 'big hooray' today, too." Second helpings, "pass this," and "pass that" followed. "Oohs" and "aahs" surrounded Maggie like echoes bouncing off a dry cavern wall.

"Every year is better than before," Aunt Minnie said. "And the carrots are perfect, my dear."

"Yeah, Mom. It rocks." Samantha's dwindling portion should have made Maggie proud. Her sixteen-year-old finicky eater had no complaints at all. "Mom, you all right?"

Maggie sensed them all staring. Like a perfectly browned turkey, her juices ran near the surface. Tears threatened. She choked them down with a nibble of buttered bread.

"You should get more rest, dear," Aunt Minnie, who never lent a hand in the kitchen, said as she scooped a giant serving of sweet potatoes onto her plate, dropping a slippery pecan on the tablecloth.

David said, "Hey, Mags, I could Cajun-fry us a turkey for Christmas if it would help." He winked at Maggie. She turned down his offer every year.

"Eww." Samantha wrinkled her nose. "In grease? I don't think so. Uncle Earnest and I care about things like that, don't we? Yuck."

David pointed a fork at Samantha. "Don't knock it till you've tried it, Sammy."

Maggie laid her napkin on the table and rose. "I'm done. Through." The browned turkey image remained.

Pop tried to seat her with a restraining hand. "Why, you haven't eaten a thing. Don't leave yet. The dishes can wait."

"I mean I'm through with Thanksgiving, Pop."

Maggie kept her voice steady though her knees quaked.

"Well, of course you are," Aunt Minnie said. "All the work's been done."

Maggie glanced around her family member's picked-over plates, a still life of Americans with eyes bigger than stomachs. Thanksgiving—a time to feast, to indulge, and to sacrifice the fatted cook.

Well, this cook's had it!

Maggie eyed the captive, overstuffed family lounging around her table. "I've roasted twenty-some-odd turkeys through the years; peeled and boiled no telling how many carrots; baked and mashed sweet potatoes till I'm pulp, made countless pies from scratch, and giblet gravy no one eats but David." She stopped to draw a breath.

"I'm sure the gravy's wonderful, Maggie," Aunt Minnie said. "You know we all love your cooking."

"You love it so much, you've come to expect it. Well, no more. I resign." Maggie fled the room, feeling like she'd just performed a scene from Turkey Bird's Nightmare on Maggie Street.

She cupped one ear at the kitchen door, hoping to hear them agree the holiday was too much for her. She envisioned a helpful family gathered around the kitchen sink instead of the usual: another miraculous dishrag touchdown for Maggie—38 dishes to ZERO help.

Everyone remained still until David said, in a voice that defied *her* reality *and* imagination, "O. . .kay. Can I interest anyone in some pie and football? I'm sure Maggie made coffee."

Chapter 4

Maggie pried and scraped at the crusted drippings that clung to the greasy roaster, but only managed to splash filthy dishwater on her blouse. *Errrr!* She threw a discarded dryer sheet into the pan to loosen the mess—a trick she'd learned from a magazine at the pediatrician's office—unlocked the back door, and set the roaster in the slush on the porch. She'd dare anyone to bring the thing in before next year.

Back inside, Maggie drummed her fingers on the counter. Aunt Minnie would lie down to recuperate from "stuffing herself silly." Earnest would join David, Charlie, Pop, and the boys around the television to offer reverence and holy shouts of encouragement to the sports gods they loved. Samantha would amuse her young girl cousins with stories of guys and makeovers until she tired of their company. Brophy needed a nap.

So did Maggie. But she had a strict personal policy against rest. She poured herself a pick-me-up and sipped the hazelnut coffee with pleasure. With enough in her veins, she could maintain her ideal, taking-it-easy-is-for-wimps approach.

When no second-string dishwashers arrived, Maggie opened the back door and carefully stacked her dirty china on the wet porch. She hid the grimy silverware inside the roaster. *One must be practical when considering what people might steal.* Even in her frustration, she didn't want to tempt anyone.

Samson sauntered over. Maggie watched him lick the top plate. *Why did I agree to feed a stupid cat on top of everything else I have to do?* She couldn't help thinking where his tongue might have been. She bent down to retrieve the plates.

"Nice dishwasher you found." Humor lined Jill's voice.

Maggie stiffened.

Samson licked the gravy grease, avoiding tidbits left from Maggie's famous corn-pudding casserole.

Maggie felt her face grow pink before she turned around. "Uh. . ." How did one explain undisguised insanity to a new relative? "I was. . .ah. . .just. . .um. . . letting the cat have some leftovers. His owners are away on a cruise. This way I won't have to feed him later." She spit out the sentences much like her teenage daughter did when trying to cover her mischief. It never worked.

"You need to come with me." Jill's serious tone would have scared Maggie if she hadn't seen the sparkle in her sister-in-law's green eyes. Jill grinned as she held up twin cucumber slices, rescued from the dinner salad.

What in the world? Charlie married a live wire.

"I thought you'd have honeymoon-itis," Maggie said, hoping to divert the conversation away from her odd behavior. "The kind where you glue yourself to a silly football game to demonstrate your love." Maggie couldn't imagine what Jill must think, watching a cat lick her china.

"I gave that up when I got the ring." She flashed her left hand at Maggie.

Maggie whistled. She'd been so busy, she'd overlooked the gorgeous wedding set. "It's beautiful. Elegant." *Like you.*

Jill and Charlie had met and married in Hawaii. Maggie and David hadn't had the money to attend, so this was their first chance to meet the girl who'd converted the staunch bachelor of the family.

Maggie headed for familiar territory. "I've got to get these dishes done. If I wait any longer, I won't have the energy. Besides, if anyone else catches me out here with the dishes and the cat, they'll know the truth: Thanksgiving made me loopy."

"That's what these are for." Jill jiggled the cucumbers with a flick of her wrist. "Unlooping."

Maggie looked at Jill with visible doubt before shooing Samson away. When he meowed in protest, Maggie scraped some turkey scraps onto the sidewalk. Then she helped Jill cart things back inside.

Her sister-in-law began loading the dirty dishes into the dishwasher. But as soon as Jill put one in, Maggie took it out, dropping each into sudsy water where it belonged.

Jill stood to the side, observing, looking somewhat baffled. "What are you doing?"

"The dishes." Maggie didn't know what the fuss was about; she always did them this way.

"You don't have to do all that. That's what *dishwashers* are for. Have you got any more cucumber? I want a couple slices, too."

Maggie searched the refrigerator drawer and hunted down the one she'd partially cut for lunch. "Here it is, but I'm warning you; I don't eat cucumbers. The only cucumber I'm friendly with is Larry on the Veggie Tales videos." Maggie returned to scrubbing.

"Where's a knife? I'll cut us some. You're going to

love this." Jill dumped the old slices into the trash. "They're better cold anyway."

Maggie's insides were already in an uproar from being caught outside. "I really can't eat them." *They hurt my stomach.* She offered Jill a knife.

"We're not going to." Jill peeled the skin away from the cucumber. "I couldn't eat another bite if I wanted to. Everything was *so* good. I'm stuffed."

Maggie dunked dishes in the soapy water, then rearranged them in the dishwasher. "So, how'd you like your first Mackenzie Thanksgiving?"

Maggie felt her sister-in-law's eyes boring into her. She turned to see her intuition was right. *"Apologize,"* commanded an inner voice. "Sorry I ruined it."

"I'm not." Jill chuckled, clearly amused. "Finding you outside with your china let me know we could be friends. Before that, you intimidated me. I'd never want to cook this much or clean it up. I don't know how you've done it so long." Jill leaned against the counter and scrutinized Maggie. "Do you really always do your dishes that way? Prewashing them instead of just rinsing them?"

Maggie nodded, tackling a handful of silverware with a scrub brush before loading it.

"I put my dishes in with crud all over them," Jill said.

"And they come out clean?"

"*Every* time."

"I find that hard to believe." Maggie transferred the silverware to the dishwasher basket.

"Charlie said you've been catering the holidays since Ma got sick." Jill finished slicing the cucumber, then rewrapped it in plastic wrap. "That's why I worked for a cruise line. They fed me. I'm hopeless in the kitchen." Jill opened the refrigerator and stored the leftover in the drawer. "Now that I'm landlocked, I don't know what Charlie will eat. We'll both probably starve."

"Don't let Charlie fool you; he can cook." *Unlike his mother.* Maggie began scrubbing pots. "Just before our first Thanksgiving, Ma lost her mother. David and I were only dating, yet somehow I wound up cooking his great-grandmother's recipes. I don't recall being asked. I just stepped in to fill a gap and wound up a permanent replacement. David says my cooking won his heart." Maggie smiled.

She pushed a bit of hair away from her eyes with her forearm. "I should be used to it by now. I don't know why I gave that selfish little speech. I love my family. I love serving others. I even *love* to cook." Maggie shook her head. "I don't want to be self-centered."

"Phooey." Jill held a thin cucumber sliver to the light. "These work better skinny. I've only known you for a day, but *you're* not selfish. Far from it."

Maggie watched, her curiosity growing. She preferred hers cut thick for salads, even though she couldn't eat them. She couldn't imagine what Jill wanted with cucumbers.

Jill's slender hands with the perfect French-tipped nails offered some slices to Maggie. "Here."

Maggie wiped her hands on a dish towel, folded it on the counter, and stacked the slices in her palm.

Jill pointed toward the door leading to the backyard. "We need a way out of here where we don't have to cross the goal line by the TV. Or I'll get suckered in by *love.*" Jill winked and laid the knife on the counter.

Maggie placed the knife in the sink. "It's cold outside, and Brophy might need me. I can't leave. Besides, I've hardly made a dent in the mess."

"The kitchen can wait. This can't. Brophy's with Uncle Charlie. I told him to keep him busy playing horsey. He's a cute little cowboy."

Maggie tilted her head to inquire with a smile, "Charlie or Brophy?" She liked her sister-in-law already.

Jill wore the confident grin of a newlywed as she stepped outside. "I did marry a handsome cowboy, didn't I?" She motioned for Maggie to follow. "Stay close." Jill tiptoed off the porch to the sidewalk and looked both ways like a spy. She took an exaggerated step over a small puddle as if it were gigantic. With a finger pressed to her lips, she motioned for Maggie to follow.

They crept around the corner of the house, embellishing every step. Maggie kept shushing Jill. They couldn't quit laughing. Slipping in the front door, they tiptoed to the master bedroom.

Jill flopped across Maggie's bed sideways and slid two cucumber slices over her eyes. "Ahh."

Maggie joined her. The coolness felt wonderful to her tired eyelids. "This is amazing. Now I know what 'cool as a cucumber' means." She laughed way too loud over her lame pun. Maggie's long legs dangled off the bed. She pulled her feet up, knees bent. "Where'd you learn this?" She lifted one cucumber to peek at Jill.

Jill drew in a deep breath before answering, "Women's magazine. I may not cook, but I know how to use vegetables. Wait till you try the avocado facial I found."

As magnificent as the pampering felt, it didn't take long for Maggie to become restless. A thinly sliced opaque vegetable couldn't stop her from reading the family's needs listed inside her eyelids.

She sighed, knowing she should get back to work. *No rest for the mommy.*

Chapter 5

Maggie hauled herself out of bed at six the next morning, grateful for God's gift to women. *Coffee.*

While it brewed, she glanced over her morning devotional and moved on to her to-do list. The detailed record in broad neat strokes included:

1. *Feed Samson.*
2. *Christmas shop—keep Samantha in a good mood; make her feel extra-special.*
3. *David take Brophy for haircut—tell Brophy pilgrims had short hair—then to Santa for photo.*
4. *Boil turkey bones—soup.*
5. *Make turkey spaghetti—dinner.*
6. *Start Christmas decorating.*

Taking a mug of coffee, she tiptoed past her sleeping husband and placed her mug on the bathroom counter. The coffee wouldn't cool in the time it took Maggie to shower and dress.

By her second cup, she'd already boxed most of her everyday knickknacks in preparation for the decorations David would haul from the attic—if she reminded him. The turkey bones simmered on the back burner, filling the kitchen with lunch smells that made her crave leftovers. She cut a slice of pumpkin pie and topped it with whipped cream.

"Mornin', love. 'Tis the month before Christmas." David began pouring coffee.

A sharp intake of breath whistled through her clenched teeth. "Believe me, I know."

Jill walked in wearing a rosy-cheeked newlywed glow. "I usually try to get my shopping finished by August."

Maggie gave Jill a head-to-toe inspection. "Let me guess; a magazine article suggested you shop early." Jill looked like she'd just returned from the spa—shower-fresh and pretty, even in a pair of plaid sleeping pants and a yellow ducky T-shirt.

How long has it been since I glowed like that? I usually leave my prince in bed, as dead to love as an unkissed toad.

"You're going to love your Christmas present, Maggie." Jill splashed a dash of vanilla syrup into her coffee.

"David. . ." Maggie hesitated. Was it her imagination, or had a look passed between Jill and David—as if they shared a secret? "Could you. . .feed Samson for me?"

"I will. Later."

Maggie sighed. "Not later, David. Now. *Please.*"

David looked her in the eye. "It will be fine if I do it later."

"Morning, Mama." Samantha wore faded jeans and a cloud of Sun-Ripened Raspberry from Bath & Body Works, a beaded purse slung over one shoulder. "I figured the stores would open early. When're we going? I already know what I want."

Maggie rolled her eyes. "Figures. You started planning this trip last December."

"Did not." Samantha rolled her eyes in perfect imitation. "I waited until New Year's." She grinned.

Maggie opened the refrigerator and removed the 2 percent milk for Samantha's cereal. She popped off the plastic lid and said to Jill, "Today Sammy picks out and tries on everything she wants for Christmas. You're invited." Maggie reached for the Fruit Loops. "David keeps Brophy. Then, this afternoon, I go back to the mall without her to purchase as much as I can of her 'To Die For' list."

Maggie looked at her daughter with obvious pride. She enjoyed their annual shopping spree, even if it did wear her to a frazzle. The results were worth the effort: Samantha got what she wanted—her new clothes fit, the CDs were the latest, and the electronic equipment was always the right style and color. The thanks she received was the best of all. *Over the river and through the mall to the holiday I go!*

Jill whistled. "Sounds like tons of work. You're one lucky lady, Miss Samantha Jo. My mother always got me things I hid at the back of the closet." Jill poured eggnog into a glass decorated with a snowman.

Samantha gave Maggie a big hug. "Mom's pretty great." She plunged her spoon into the cereal Maggie provided.

Maggie brightened at the compliment, ready to buy Samantha the world. This day was known in the Mommy Manual as Samantha's Day, and there were many compliments ahead. Gifts spoke love to Samantha in a language she understood. Maggie turned to put the cereal away as David cleared his throat.

"Uh, I meant to tell you last night. . ."

Maggie straightened the pantry shelves, pretending they were messy. She didn't want to hear any excuses.

"I can't keep Brophy today. I promised the guys"— he meant the cousins—"I'd take them skeet shooting."

He moved to retrieve the cereal he liked from a shelf at Maggie's eye level.

They made eye contact.

She let her eyes communicate bitter disappointment. *For a man who works hard, you're a holiday goof-off.*

Maggie felt David's quick forgive-me hug and forced a pleasant smile. "Can't Brophy go along? I was counting on you." She remembered how the cousins had begged yesterday, but she hadn't figured he'd go along with their plans.

"It's too dangerous for a three-year-old."

"He needs a haircut." Maybe she could guilt him. "I needed your help with that, too."

"His hair's not in his eyes yet. Take him with you. He needs to see Santa."

Brophy entered as if on cue, his footed pajamas slapping the kitchen floor. Maggie hissed, "Shh!" at David.

"I don't wanna sit in Santy's lap." Brophy folded his arms and scowled.

Annoyed at David's insensitivity, Maggie cast him a warning glare. She'd hoped he would pick up the slack since Santa had scared the stuffings out of Brophy last year.

"You'll like Santa this year, son," David assured Brophy as he scooped him into his arms. "Hey! You're a big boy, aren't you?" David's nasty habit of mocking his children reared its head.

"I y'am." Brophy puckered his lips.

"You won't get any toys." Samantha liked nothing better than to frustrate Brophy. "You have to sit on Santa's lap to stay off the naughty list."

"I been good." Brophy kicked at her though David held him.

Maggie wrung out the sponge, frustrated that Jill had to witness all this.

"Why, you little. . ." Samantha leaned close enough to make Brophy cross-eyed and pinched his arm.

Brophy cried out, "She gave me an owie."

David dumped him into Maggie's arms. "Samantha Jo Mackenzie, you're way too old for that." He pointed toward her room.

"Me!" Indignation blossomed on her innocent face. "You're always sticking up for him like he's some kind of baby. Tell him, Mom. He bites when you're not around, Dad."

Maggie hated her children's bickering. "Don't say another word, or you'll be on my naughty list, and that doesn't bode well for a girl who wants to *see Santa today*, if you catch my drift." She hesitated long enough to compliment herself for the zinger she was about to deliver. "In fact, you're going to sit on Santa's opposite knee, holding your little brother's hand. I want a joint picture this year."

Samantha sputtered, "What? At the mall? But. . . my friends." Disbelief and humiliation mingled on her face.

David came to Maggie's defense. "Your mother said 'not another word.' Call it punishment or encouragement—whatever you like. But if you continue, I'll have Mom sign you up for a holiday job while you're at the mall." He paused—letting the initial threat sink in—and, winking at Maggie, added, "As an *elf*."

Maggie knew that one stung. While Samantha morphed into a semipleasant teenager, David smiled at Maggie. She placed Brophy on the ground, thankful for her husband.

Jill drew the pumpkin pie across the counter and cut a slice with the knife propped on the rim. "I'll be ready as soon as I have some of this and throw on some clothes. I can apply my makeup in the car." Jill added a dollop of whipped cream, delaying Samantha's trip even longer. "I *want* this recipe." Jill hooked her pinky through the topping and dashed a streak on Maggie's forehead before she could protest.

Before Maggie knew what came over her, she'd poked Jill's pie and smeared pumpkin on Jill's cheek. She hardly recognized herself today.

Maggie glanced at Brophy. "Sorry, son. Mommy shouldn't have acted that way."

Jill rubbed the pie into her skin like moisturizer. "We'll see if this works as well as the forty-dollar stuff I bought last week." She laughed. "It's called Pumpkin-A-Peel. The enzymes remove dead skin cells and make your skin feel tingly."

Maggie opened the bottom bin of the fridge and tossed the leftover cucumber Jill's way. "Merry Christmas, facial girl."

"Merry to you, too." Jill faked a pout. "You *know* what your problem is, don't you?" Jill tossed the cucumber back in Maggie's direction while Brophy stared wide-eyed. "You don't subscribe to any magazines."

"That's not a problem," David said. "There's no money for extras." He opened a sales circular. He'd made it his job to find the best holiday buys, frequently telling Samantha she should get more for their money.

"Too bad," Jill said. "Magazines are the ticket to joining the Facial Girls' Sisterhood."

Maggie sighed. "David's right; I *don't* have the money. *Or* the time." She pitched Samantha's plastic cereal bowl into the dishwasher. "I can barely get my Bible reading done each morning; then it's go, go, go till bedtime." She indicated her open planner on the counter. "That thing has a life of its own. Pampering isn't for me."

Jill placed an encouraging hand on Maggie's shoulder. "*Your* choice."

Chapter 6

"M om, you missed the turn. This isn't the way to the mall," Samantha called from behind her, having been relegated to the backseat of the minivan with Brophy due to Jill's riding shotgun.

Maggie glanced at Jill. Did she know what she'd started? The seedling had been planted by her random "your choice" comment and could only thrive without guilt, so Maggie drove without looking at Samantha.

"Mom, did you hear me? You went the wrong way."

Maggie stayed calm. "You're very observant."

"I'm *not* looking for clothes anywhere except the mall, no matter what Daddy says." Panic rose in the teenager's voice.

"I'm not asking you to." The scowl Maggie saw when she glanced in the rearview mirror almost turned the minivan around. She hated opposition.

Before she could renege, she said, "I'm looking for some magazine ideas to destress our holidays. It shouldn't take long. Maybe I'll even find something on how to change a sourpuss into a sugarplum." Maggie turned and smiled her brightest, hoping to transform the frown on Samantha's face.

"*Mom!*" Samantha moaned like a teenaged drama queen. "This is *my* day, not yours."

"It's everybody's day, Sammy. Where's your Christmas spirit?" Maggie attempted to sound sunny, though a chill wind threatened to scatter her plans.

She parked the van in the nearest vacant space—a mile from Wal-Mart's front doors. Maggie unlatched Brophy's child restraint, then focused on her headstrong daughter. "I need a change, Samantha. I'm looking for a way to transform Christmas from 'gimme-gimme' to. . . oh. . .I don't know what. . . ." Despair and defeat landed with rock-solid footing. *Who am I trying to kid? I probably can't change, even if I want to.* Maggie heard the familiar tinkle of holiday bell ringers in the background. *Gimme—gimme—gimme,* they announced charity-style.

"This isn't fair!" Samantha looked at her aunt as they neared the store. "She and Dad dreamed this up." It was obvious Samantha wanted to draw her aunt into the argument, but Jill continued walking and sorting the contents of her purse. Samantha fumed. "I'll never buy clothes at Wal-Mart like Mom."

"This isn't about you." Maggie offered the stiff girl a one-armed hug. *Every time I try to do something for myself, my family goes ballistic.*

"My point exactly." Samantha pulled away. "You know you can't go in here without filling a basket." The automatic doors parted.

Maggie said, "I'm looking for a better way to manage Christmas." *Something has to change, and it had better be me.*

"I wanna see the toys," Brophy said, delighted by the prospects inside the stadium-sized store. Brophy yanked Samantha's hand, ready to run. "Come on, Sissy."

"Wait, Brophy." Maggie trudged behind, the energy robbed from her heartfelt desire. How would she ever change Christmas if she couldn't even maneuver a stubborn teenager?

Jill accepted a shopping cart from the door greeter and turned it toward the magazine aisle as if she hadn't heard a single unpleasant thing. "What did we do before we could buy panties, hunting gear, and toys in the same store?" She didn't look at mother or daughter.

They moved past an in-house bank, a photo developer, and the optical department. Cashiers' machines *ka-chinged* all around them as shoppers prepared to depart with buggy loads of bulging blue plastic bags. They passed the Angel Tree, an evergreen decorated with the names and needs of impoverished children in the area.

Maggie slowed. *Perhaps we should shop for an Angel Tree child instead.* It would teach her children a valuable lesson about what the season was really all about—not mother or daughter, but a baby named Jesus. But before she could stop, Brophy darted for the toy section. "Samantha, keep an eye on your brother. And don't lose him."

Samantha followed at a calculated distance.

Jill chuckled. "Everything's so spread out, they ought to add aerobics to their advertising slogan. Falling prices and lower pounds *guaranteed.*"

Maggie eyed her thin companion, glad for the subject change. "I'm not sure about the pounds part, but there *is* one thing they don't advertise—the miscellaneous stuff we can hide in a grocery bill. It's dangerous when you can go in for a dozen eggs and come out with a TV." The children were many aisles away, and she felt the relief. "Here's what I need." Maggie reached for the magazine *Real Simple* from the abundant selection on the racks in front of them. She loved the photographs and features. "It's a bit pricey." She tossed it into the basket. "But it looks like a great way to simplify things."

Jill placed a hand on Maggie's arm. "I hope I haven't

steered you in the wrong direction." Concern lined Jill's voice and wrinkled her brow. "Tackling the holidays in a different way could prove more stressful than doing things like you always have. And it might cost more money." Jill's mouth twisted with unease.

"You think I'm doing the wrong thing, too?" Maggie heaved a sigh as her mood swung from newly excited to typically discouraged. "I didn't think you'd disapprove." She groaned. "I should have gone shopping with Samantha as planned, shouldn't I? Let her have her way. I mean. . .day." Maggie squeezed her eyes shut and rubbed her temples. "How could I be *so* selfish?"

"Whoa. Slow down." Jill patted her firmly on the back as though she were a deflated exercise ball in need of a good pumping. "It's not like you're swearing off Christmas or anything. You're not trying to skip it. Just make it a little saner. Take a deep breath." Jill demonstrated.

Maggie followed.

"Good. And another." Jill breathed deep and exhaled through pursed lips. "Now let's see what we can find." Jill pointed to a teaser entitled "Diet Mistakes." "I don't need that one. I like Cheetos. Eat them every chance I get."

"That was *real simple.*" Maggie snickered at her pun. She picked up a magazine on home decorating, easily discarding it. "I'd have to start from scratch. It'd be like redoing a bargain basement. Way off the stress charts."

"Your home is what I call homespun charming."

"Don't open any doors. I hid the junk in the closets."

"Here's an article you might like." Jill opened to a page promising ways to unstuff Christmas.

Maggie glanced over her shoulder. "Hmm. How to get everyone involved in preparing the meal. Wouldn't that be something? Toss it in the basket." The next magazine promised "Homecomings to Remember," and she flipped it atop the other glossy covers in her cart. "Oh, and put in the one over there about simplifying stress. I've got to read that."

"This one includes make-ahead recipes, a Christmas countdown, and photos. See?" Jill held it out.

"I'll take it," Maggie said without looking. She began laughing. "Here's a quote from Franklin D. Roosevelt that fits the Mackenzie clan: 'Sometimes the best way to keep peace in the family is to keep the members of the family apart for a while.'"

Humor danced in Jill's eyes. "Are you asking me to go?" She tossed a cooking magazine in the general direction of the others. "I can't. You're stuck with me."

As newlyweds, Charlie and Jill were in the process of building their first home, Maggie knew, but all of a sudden Jill sounded like the other relatives. They all wanted to stay. With Maggie! "Maybe I should leave it open on the coffee table." Spite crossed Maggie's face, but then she looked at her feet as guilt snaked up her spineless back. "I shouldn't have said that. Sometimes I think I'll go nuts, but then I'm glad Sammy and Brophy get the chance to know their older relatives. Some kids don't. I try to count my blessings." She hoped she didn't sound like a martyr.

"Spoken like a true Thanksgiving Day leftover!" Jill smirked.

Whoops.

Jill picked up another magazine and started thumbing through. "Speak of the devil. Here's one with your name written all over it—'All You Need for Christmas is a Stress-Free Season.'"

"Hand it over." Maggie turned to an article titled "Managing Difficult Personalities."

"Speaking of the relatives—" Maggie began to skim. She'd needed this one yesterday!

"Definitely buy that one, and I'll read it, too." Jill took it from her and laid it on top of the others.

"Let's walk to the checkout counters. There're more up there. And we need to page Samantha." Maggie envisioned the loudspeaker summons and Samantha's unhappy response. *Another confrontation.* "She'll die a thousand deaths."

"Maybe we ought to page Brophy instead."

"Much better plan. Thanks." Maggie pushed the cart toward checkout. "How many articles do you think we've found?"

"Seven or eight."

"I want one for every day between now and Christmas—that makes twenty-eight. Oh, rats. I forgot. File folders to organize them." She turned the buggy toward stationery.

"Whoa. If you read them too close to Christmas, they won't do any good. I'm warning you. Choosing not to be like you've always been is like walking uphill backwards."

Maggie wished she'd taken her antacid. "Our Sunday school teacher claims, 'Choosing to do what you've always done while expecting different results is the equivalent of insanity.'"

Jill walked along, flipping pages. "I don't guess your teacher would like this one." She showed Maggie what she'd found—"Santa's Tavern: The Guide to Mixing the Perfect Holiday Drink."

With her conservative-evangelical roots exposed, the innocent comment pricked like a dart. Maggie stopped midaisle, causing the lady behind her to almost bump into them. She moved to let the woman pass, then asked Jill, "Do you think it's too worldly to try to change

Christmas this way? I mean, these aren't exactly articles about the baby Jesus." She pointed to the top title on the stack, "Six Keys to a More Rambunctious Sex Life," and blushed. "They're not Christian magazines."

"So the real world has nothing to offer *Christians?*" Jill raised an eyebrow. "I think self-help articles are something Christians should approve of—part of finding an abundant life."

Maggie didn't have an argument for that, though she knew it wasn't what Christ meant. She didn't know her sister-in-law well. *I guess I shouldn't have assumed Jill was a Christian.*

Maggie turned toward the pharmacy. "I'm going to find some antacids. Then it's on to the mall."

Chapter 7

At the mall, Brophy had screamed at Santa as Maggie predicted, and Samantha had shopped till Maggie dropped. But Maggie had caught holiday fever yesterday as surely as she'd catch the flu bug later this season. This morning she ached, and her bank account needed a pain reliever, but she was ready to decorate.

Yesterday's to-dos hadn't been done. The tree wasn't up, and they'd shared a bucket of Tasty Cluck for dinner instead of the turkey spaghetti she'd planned, but all in all, she'd accomplished a lot.

She poured a cup of coffee and grabbed her Bible and planner. Jill was convinced the magazine project would bring Maggie ready answers to de-stressing. But how could man-made advice bring joy to a holiday that revolved around the divine?

Maggie pushed the magazines aside, took her planner, and moved yesterday's to-dos to today's list. She read from the book of Psalms for a while, glad for the uninterrupted time, then went to find Mr. Claus.

She needed help with the tree—although trying to get David to fluff the smashed artificial branches would be equivalent to keeping Brophy's magnet letters on the refrigerator door when it slammed.

Maggie found David where she expected to, sitting in a recliner, listening to football on the radio. "Can't we do it later?" he asked between plays.

She posed like a referee—nonnegotiable with hands low on hips. "No," she said. And it worked.

David cheered the unseen football players on the radio. Though he ignored Maggie, he kept working, and she accepted it as a fair compromise. Every once in a while, as they sorted and inserted branches, she had to explain things like, "That branch doesn't work in that spot," or "Let's shove the tree six inches to the left."

And he would say, "Too bad we can't earn frequent flyer miles from all the talking you do. I can hardly listen to the game with all your chatter."

When it came time to add lights, he threw a penalty flag. "Who sees the back side anyway? The window faces the yard."

"You sound like Samantha, always trying to stop

me from doing things right." It would take them both standing on separate ladders and cooperating to string lights around the tree. His attitude annoyed her, but she kept working.

"Speaking of Samantha, where is the princess?"

"I sent her to the store for more lights." Maggie stood back to survey the eight-foot tree. Thanks to her efforts, the top section was lit. Maggie climbed the ladder and leaned toward the tree, steadying herself with one hand against the wall. She balanced the wobbly angel. "Is it straight? . . . Honey? . . . David, did I get it straight?"

"Hmm?" He held the ladder with one hand, his eyes glued to the radio on the floor.

"Can you *see* them if you concentrate?" Maggie climbed down one step and leaned back. She hoped David had hold of the ladder.

"Hmm? What? Did you say something?" David glanced up. "Careful, hon. Don't fall."

As if because of his prediction, Maggie tumbled into David's arms. She shut her eyes, expecting a sweet kiss of relief.

"No! Aw, come on!" David stomped his foot. He put her down with the gentleness of a linebacker. "I can't believe that ref."

She glared at him but he didn't notice. "It isn't like

any of *this* matters." She indicated the light cords strewn around the den.

"Oh, honey, I'm so glad you understand." David gave her a genuine hug, then retreated with his game to the bedroom.

She glared after him. *I'd like to take that radio and punt it out of the stadium!* What was so hard about listening to something distracting *while* working? Mothers did it all the time.

Maggie plopped down on a kitchen chair and flipped through a magazine left on the table, anger washing over her. *How dare he? It isn't like I asked him for anything hard. Why does everyone treat me this way?*

She tore out articles whether she needed them or not. "Four Quick Cures for Stress"; "Creating a Day You'll Treasure"; "Homecomings to Remember"; "New Twists on Tradition"; "Make-Ahead Recipes"; and "Simplify Your Holidays." Maybe if she read them, she could ignore the stress.

Samantha fluttered in, dropped a Wal-Mart sack on the counter where it would stay until Maggie moved it, and opened the refrigerator door. "What's to eat?"

"Whatever you want." Maggie stapled an article into a folder.

"Thanks, Mom. I'll take grilled cheese."

"The pan's over there. It's time you put your

home-economics skills to use."

"Mo—om," Samantha moaned as if Maggie had asked her to scoop doggy poop.

Before guilt could stop her, Maggie blurted, "I'm in the middle of a project here. The cheese is in the refrigerator drawer. You'll find the bread second shelf down in the pantry." Maggie pulled her Bible close. She hesitated before adding, "I'd like one, too." Maggie felt Samantha's astonishment before she looked. Samantha stood like a statue frozen by the escaping refrigerated air.

Maggie moved to the den, carrying her project along. A box of decorations awaited her attention. She ignored it as she folded herself onto the couch and reached for a magazine. She stopped and opened the Bible where she could glance over a verse or two. Multitasking made her feel better.

Jill surprised her by rounding the corner, and Maggie quickly covered her Bible with a magazine.

"Something to hide?" Jill asked.

"You startled me." Maggie cringed at the conviction she'd hidden her faith. "I was working on our project."

"Good. You need some veggie time."

The frying pan clanged against a burner, followed by the sizzling of melting butter. "I was going to ask Samantha to help me decorate, but I set her to making sandwiches instead. She has a bad habit of keeping me off track with questions like. . ." Maggie mimicked, " 'Wouldn't this look better over there? Let's not do this now. We need some new decorations; let's go shopping. Do we have to put garlands everywhere? Can we take a break now? Who sees this anyway? Someone needs to if we're going to this much trouble. Why don't you throw *me* a party?' "

"Sounds like a decorating party pooper. I'll help. I can't wait till Charlie and I have a place of our own."

A spark in Maggie's mind burst into a flaming thought that made Maggie burn with guilt: *I can't wait till you move either.* The instantaneous wildfire turned her cheeks pink. *Lord, I'm sorry. I don't know where that thought came from. I want to be generous, especially at Christmastime.*

Jill picked a magazine, plopped down beside Maggie, and started turning pages at leisure. "I see you've made a good start on your project."

Maggie gathered the stapler, scissors, and scraps. She restacked the magazines and placed the clippings in folders.

Jill faked a cough. "You're kicking up dust. Tell your overworked brain to be still." Jill's smile reached her eyes.

A glossy cover caught Maggie's attention. Rustling pages swished in Jill's hand. Butter sizzled in the kitchen as Samantha flipped a grilled-cheese sandwich.

Maggie moved Jill's feet off the coffee table. "It's time to tackle a *real* holiday project—making this place look like Christmas." She plucked thick white polyester batting from a plastic bag and formed fluffy hills and flatlands, then positioned a Christmas village on the "snow." She called to Samantha, "Put another grilled cheese on for Aunt Jill."

"There's nothing like the smell of burned cheese to make you hungry," Jill joked.

"I didn't want you to feel left out." The smile had returned to Maggie's voice.

Jill positioned the mirrored pond and skaters. "This is so pretty. Charlie and I don't have any decorations yet. What's next?"

"The manger scene." Maggie moved across the room toward the piano. "You almost done in there, Samantha?"

No answer.

"You want me to go see what's keeping her?" Jill asked.

"No, leave her alone. I haven't got time to eat anyway." Maggie cleared away Samantha's sheet music and replaced it with a doily. "There's one good thing about decorating. There's no room left for clutter when I get done." Maggie drew the Mary figurine from the box, followed by Joseph.

Jill looked into the deep cardboard box. "I can't believe you use all this."

"It's Christmas. This is how I help others celebrate." Maggie fingered the baby Jesus. "Everyone would be disappointed if I didn't. But. . ." Maggie hated feeling so downhearted.

Jill walked to the couch and brought back the magazines. She fanned them out with a raised brow. The covers practically twinkled with clever promises.

Maggie sighed. "It took designers and writers weeks to create those pages, and I'm only one person. I don't think that's the answer." She turned the baby figurine in her hand, then placed Jesus beneath Mary's and Joseph's watchful eyes. *This used to be the best part of Christmas.*

Something about setting out the manger scene yesterday had Maggie brooding this morning. She'd dreamed she'd lost the Christ child figurine, and no one in the family could find Him.

After a quick check over her planner and a final swig of coffee, Maggie reached for her Bible. Having been reminded by a Christian women's magazine article on holiday stress, she began reading about Martha and Mary, two of Jesus' friends. Martha cooked a meal all by herself while her sister, Mary, sat at Jesus' feet and worshiped Him. Martha complained and asked Jesus to make Mary help her.

It wasn't hard for Maggie to identify with Martha. *That's how my trouble began—by taking on too much responsibility. But You made me like Martha, God. You know that. You take pleasure in all I accomplish, don't You?*

She glanced back at the Bible. A verse flew off the page like a missile aimed for her heart. *"Martha, Martha, you are worried and upset about many things, but only one thing is needed. Mary has chosen what is better."*

God had gone to meddling. The verse might as well have read: Maggie, Maggie, you are worried and upset about many things. *Come on, God. You know I don't want to worry. I want to worship You. I'll get this under control, Lord, really I will.*

Resolved to get "Martha" some help, Maggie dragged out a notepad and wrote:

Dear Family,

As you know, Thanksgiving wore me to the wishbone. I will NOT be cooking the entire meal all by myself this Christmas.

Choose a casserole or gelatin salad to put in containers that can be thrown away. (Jill will tell you—this is for my sanity. She doesn't want to find me outside with dirty dishes again. Ask

Jill—a funny story.) Only fix what the sixteen of us can eat. My waistline tells me we won't need leftovers.

While I enjoy rave reviews, I don't think the Lord deserves table-scrap thanks in a hasty prayer. Maybe this way God will get the praise He deserves, and we can spread the compliments around to some other cooks.

Hip-hooray! Love,
Maggie (better known as Martha)

P.S. If you don't fix it, I guess we won't eat.

Now she had new worries. Should she include recipe cards for the family? Or let them figure out how to prepare everything without her input? She wondered if she'd enjoy relinquishing ownership and control of the fancy meal. But surely this would be her ticket to becoming more like Mary.

The phone rang.

"Maggie, it's Anne. Did I catch you at a bad time?"

My sister could bring the fruitcake and maybe some gourmet coffee since she's long distance. . . .

"Oh, Maggie. I'm glad you're home. The boys and I need. . .well, we'd like to come stay with you awhile. At least till Christmas, if that'd be all right."

"I'm afraid there's no room in the inn, Anne." Maggie finally had a reason to be thankful for her full house. "We're bursting at the seams." Anne's seven-year-old twins, Blake and Baxter, weren't the kind of angels Maggie wanted decking her halls.

"It'll only be a few weeks. Until. . .I just need some time away." Anne moved from ever-so-slight pleading to a cheerier tone. "Your house is always so fun over the holidays. We could call it an early Christmas present. Time together."

Maggie decided there must be a sign over her front door—Mackenzie Bed-and-Breakfast—full service, low rates, ten meals a day.

"I could help you cook."

Anne couldn't cook noodles without a recipe. A solid no formed in Maggie's mind, but she heard herself say, "If you *really* need to. I guess we'll manage." Samantha would hate the couch, but something had to be wrong for Anne to return so suddenly.

"I knew you'd agree." Relief crossed the phone line, adding to Maggie's suspicion. "Our plane lands in two hours. Could you pick us up at the airport? Thanks, Maggie. Gotta go."

Maggie heard the flight attendant instruct those traveling with small children to board, right before the line went dead. She leapt from the couch, straightening pillows and magazines in a whirlwind. Here she'd been praying to become more like Mary, and now "Martha's" workload had suddenly tripled. She looked toward the ceiling. *Thanks a lot.*

Chapter 8

Maggie watched Anne enter the main terminal, a leopard-print tote slung over her shoulder, twin boys flanking her pencil-thin frame, and her blond hair swinging. With megabucks to spend, Anne's gift was shopping, not serving. Not once had she helped Maggie. She just arrived bearing gifts like some benevolent Mrs. Claus without the rosy cheeks or plump behind.

As she neared, Maggie noticed exhaustion in Anne's eyes. Anne, who usually offered a superficial peck and less than intimate hug, fell into Maggie's arms for several seconds. Then she reached for Samantha.

Samantha received her usual kiss-kiss. "Why'd you come so early?"

Anne looked at Maggie over Samantha's head. "I

thought it'd be a nice surprise. I can help your mother with Christmas this way."

Tears shimmered on Anne's lashes. Blake and Baxter skittered to the nearest newspaper stand where they clamored over licorice and gummy worms.

"No need to pay inflated prices. We can stop for candy on the way home," Maggie offered.

"I'm sure you have better things to do with your time." Anne paid for the boys' candy.

Maggie bristled. "You have a nice flight? Samantha, take your aunt's bag."

Anne gave it over without argument. "The flight was fine. Good weather."

Maggie noticed the heavy coat over Anne's arm. "Was it cold at home this morning?"

"Very chilly," Anne answered, as if Maggie had posed a question with a double meaning.

"We had snow here last week. Not what *you'd* consider snow, but enough for Brophy to feel like he got to see some. It melted off by noon. Oh, I forgot." Maggie held her hand to her mouth. "You were here." She wasn't trying to be funny. The week seemed far away with Anne arriving off schedule.

"It's strange, isn't it?" Anne remained expressionless, staring across the terminal. ". . .how things work out." She fished around in her red leather purse. "I miss my favorite niece and sister all year long; then I see them twice in a row." Anne smiled as if her emotions had returned to normal. She held up two baggage claim tickets stapled to an envelope.

Maggie could only stare.

Anne usually traveled with a stockpile of luggage, even if she only spent the night. Instead, she retrieved two slim bags and proclaimed, "I packed pretty quickly. We'll have to go shopping."

Samantha grinned at the suggestion, then asked what Maggie also wondered, "How long are you staying?"

"Till Christmas."

"What about Uncle John?"

"Has to work."

Maggie noticed she didn't say he'd join them for Christmas. Anne and John were obviously having marital problems. But it wasn't hard for Anne to avoid an answer since no one asked the question.

"Boys, don't run," Anne called the identical blond boys back to her side.

Samantha looked from boy to boy. "I still can't tell them apart."

When they arrived at Maggie's house, Jill threw the front door open. "Anne, it's good to see you." The aroma of gingerbread and sugar cookies greeted them. Jill had lit scented candles.

As Maggie passed by, Jill caught her arm and whispered, "Why is it when you decide to slow down, life accelerates? All the more reason you'll love your Christmas present."

"What is it?"

"You must have been pretty nice this year." Jill winked.

"I'm going to rest a bit." Anne announced, then headed for Samantha's room, entered, and closed the door as they watched.

"What if I need something?" Samantha asked, dismayed.

"You'll have to wait." Maggie lowered her voice. "She looks like she hasn't slept in a week."

Jill agreed. "She looks terrible. I think I'll grab a few winks myself."

Baxter tugged on Samantha's hand. "Where's your PlayStation?"

"You know we don't have one," Samantha said without hiding her irritation.

Blake frowned. "Then what are we supposed to do?"

Samantha flipped on the television and handed Baxter the remote. "We have cable. Knock yourself out."

Maggie rolled her eyes. *How am I supposed to monitor*

them and still get everything done?

"Samantha, see that they don't watch the wrong channel."

"Why me?"

"Why not you?"

"They're not my responsibility."

"And they're mine?" Maggie whispered, hands on her hips. She glanced at Blake and Baxter to confirm they weren't listening. "They look content enough with the Disney Channel; just check on them now and then."

Samantha stormed toward her room, remembered Anne, then turned into the master suite—the only unoccupied room in the house.

In the kitchen, Samantha's dirty oatmeal bowl sat beside the remains of David's peanut butter-chocolate smoothie concoction, which had dried on the blender. Jill and Charlie had apparently gone shopping while she'd been at the airport, then returned with overflowing sacks and dropped them next to the unopened Christmas cards and winter garb littering the counter. Everyone had used two or three glasses or mugs and hadn't bothered to rinse them. Her kitchen resembled a yard sale.

In the living room, Maggie plopped down beside Baxter, grabbed a magazine, and started thumbing at speed-reader pace. The whole family expected her to clean, organize, dispense, and arrange their life. *Well, they can forget it. This elf's had it.*

"Looks like you need my favorite cure—a bubble bath," Jill said.

Maggie hadn't moved from the couch, and she'd grown drowsy from the effort of procrastinating.

"I'll go run the water. You got any bubble bath?"

Maggie yawned and stretched, sorry to be roused. "Brophy has some. Where is he, by the way? If he's quiet, he's probably in trouble." She started to stand.

"Stay seated. David said you needed a break. He and Charlie took Brophy fishing. I'll be right back."

Jill returned with three bottles, a green and pink tube of some unknown substance, and a lavender-scented candle. "Pick your favorite bubble-bath aroma: Sweet Attraction, Love Spoken, or Vanilla Romance." She squeezed each bottle under Maggie's nose.

Maggie took three luxurious whiffs. Her eyes closed as she compared the subtle floral selections against the decidedly vanilla fragrance. "I'll take Vanilla Romance." Maggie watched Jill scramble through the end table drawer, searching for something. *This is craziness.*

Jill held up a matchbook with a victorious grin. "I'll start the water."

Maggie panicked. She hadn't had time to clean her bathroom. She stood to intercept. "That's okay. I can run my own tub."

"Sit. I'm happy to do it for you." Jill headed toward the hall.

Maggie blocked Jill's path, reminding herself of a football player. "It's a mess. David leaves everything out."

Jill pushed past her. "It's not like I haven't seen underwear on the floor. I worked a cruise ship. Remember?"

Maggie followed like a zombie. *A bubble bath in the middle of a day is a fantasy. I must be dreaming.*

In no time at all, Maggie found herself lounging amid popping, fragile bubbles with a gooey pink watermelon facial lathered across her cheeks, chin, and forehead. When the door burst open, she ducked for cover, expecting Brophy.

"Thought you might like some magazines." Jill laid them on the tub's edge. "Too bad you don't have a whirlpool," she said as she left.

Maggie leaned her neck against the cool tub rim and wiggled her toes through the bubbles. She had to admit it; pampering herself felt wonderful. The lavender candle, vanilla bubbles, and watermelon mask enveloped her in an aromatic cloud. But when she closed her eyes to savor the pleasure, her mind refused to relax.

She'd always organized her life around the family,

so why the sudden need to change? And how much additional stress would accompany *not* being in charge? Maybe she should make a New Year's resolution to do Christmas different *next* year.

She piled bubbles on her stomach and chest, dipped her chin in the foam, and inhaled the sweet vanilla. Any peace she'd hoped to find had disappeared. She couldn't even hear the distant echo of her dreams.

The candle flickered. What did she want? Solitude. Time to relax. Time with David. And the children. The ability to say no. Clean closets. Neat drawers. A fully decorated house. Exercise. Money to eat out more. Without weight gain. Peace.

Maggie's to-do list appeared unbidden in her mind. The Christmas Day meal had been redistributed only to be replaced by an additional three mouths to feed. Brophy sang at church tonight.

She bolted upright. *Oh my!* Water sloshed over the edge of the tub to the floor.

Maggie bounded from the tub as though the water had scalded her. She checked the clock by the sink. Brophy's choir rehearsal began in twenty minutes! And she'd forgotten the cookies she'd promised to bake. She grabbed the first article of clothing she could put her hands on—her husband's threadbare bathrobe—and tied the sash as she rammed her feet into her fuzzy slippers.

Where had the afternoon gone? And where had David taken Brophy? Jill had only said "fishing."

Bubbles clung to the tips of her hair and ears as she ran toward the kitchen. "Jill, where did they go? Did they walk or drive?"

Jill stared at the holey bathrobe. "They walked. What's the big deal?"

"Go down the street, that way." Maggie pointed north. "Run to the end of the block and turn left. It's an emergency! At the second pasture, turn right and crawl over the locked gate. Then follow the road to the end, and you'll come to a big pond where you'll find them. Tell 'em to get home *right away*."

"End of the street, left, up two pastures, then right over the gate."

Maggie nodded. "Hurry."

"What's the emergency?"

"Brophy needs to be at church in fifteen minutes with cookies in hand for his choir." Maggie flipped the oven to 350 degrees.

"So stop and buy cookies on the way. Or better yet, can't he miss it? It's only preschool choir."

"They're counting on him. He's one of the little lambs. Please hurry." Maggie wrung her hands. "I can't believe I forgot." *If Anne hadn't come home unexpectedly, I wouldn't have.*

Maggie checked the clock. It'd take Jill ten minutes to get there and back, just long enough to slice and bake the dough she'd bought for emergencies such as this. *Good planning.*

The self-proclaimed queen of fast mastered her element. Forget about frosting the cookies with white chocolate as planned. She could make three-circled snowmen faster than a blizzard could dump a foot of snow, then sprinkle them with powdered sugar with seconds to spare.

Anne emerged from a nap, looking somewhat refreshed. "What's the noise about? You could wake the dead. And what's that stuff smeared all over your face?"

"Watermelon facial Jill talked me into. There isn't time to wash it off. I forgot I've got to make cookies for Brophy's choir," Maggie said, breathless. "Hand me a cookie sheet from that cabinet." She pointed.

Anne did so, and Maggie practically threw the dough circles onto the pan. She joined each set of three into fat snowmen bound for the soon-to-be-fiery furnace. She rammed the cookie sheet into the oven before it could preheat, spinning the timer to nine. *Make that eight.* Then cranked the temperature up to 400 degrees.

If she made every traffic light between here and the church, she'd have half a minute to spare. Besides, everyone expected her to be late.

"Where are they?" Maggie fumed as she marched around the kitchen, throwing mugs and dirty dishes into the dishwasher without rinsing. When the bathrobe threatened to come loose, she cinched it tighter. "Jill should have found them by now."

Anne stared as if Maggie had lost her mind. Maggie knew Anne would never, ever leave the bathroom looking such a fright.

"Surely they took the four-wheelers. Come on. Come on." Maggie willed her son and husband toward the house as she pulled back the curtain.

Nowhere. They weren't anywhere in sight.

She ran to the front door to check. Behind her, she overheard Chevy Chase's voice. The twins had the television tuned to *National Lampoon's Christmas Vacation* where Chevy's character, Clark Griswold Jr. announced, "Nobody's walking out on this fun, old-fashioned family Christmas. No, no! We're all in this together. This is a full-blown, four-alarm holiday emergency here!"

A fitting description for a Mackenzie Christmas if Maggie had ever heard one. She looked back out the window and saw Jill sprinting toward the house. *Thank goodness.*

She readjusted the lapels of the bathrobe to cover

her cleavage and stuck her facial-masked head out the door. "Did you find them?"

Huffing and panting, Jill bent over, her hands on her thighs. "Call 9-1-1!" She gasped for air.

"Who's hurt?"

"Just do it, Maggie. Hurry!"

Chapter 9

M aggie's hand trembled as she dialed 9-1-1.
What should she tell the operator?

Jill yanked the phone from her hand.
"Go get some clothes on, then go. . ." She pointed
toward the door. "Yes, we need an ambulance," she told
the operator, then told Maggie, "Go to the pond."

Maggie yanked her fake fur coat from the hall closet.
Forcing her arms into the sleeves shoved David's robe
into twin wads around her shoulders. Without stopping
to adjust the uncomfortable mess, she raced out the
door. She had to find out what happened.

Maggie ran. Her fuzzy slippers flapped. A brisk
wind kicked up the front of the coat, reminding her
she fled nearly naked.

Up the block. Around the bend. Her legs churned.
Her head pounded. Her lungs burned. She threw herself

over the fence like a Greek hurdler, then sprinted to the pond, clasping the robe and coat with one hand.

Her throat caught when she saw him on the ground. She forgot about her appearance.

David and Charlie surrounded Brophy like angels on bent knee. "Don't move, son," she heard David caution. "Mommy's here." David looked at her in relief; then his brow rose as he surveyed her gooey pink face, bare legs, and *his* robe poking out beneath her coat.

"Brophy!" She collapsed beside him, then looked at David. "What happened?" Her hand on Brophy's chest assured her he was still breathing. As he lay pale and helpless, tears trickled down his cheeks onto the dry grass.

David answered, "We were wrestling, and I threw him over my shoulder. He landed on his back. At first, I thought he had the breath knocked out of him." David's mournful eyes communicated gut-wrenching fear.

Maggie focused on Brophy. "Tell Mommy what hurts."

"Nuttin'. I can't feel my legs." Her rambunctious little soldier wasn't moving.

"Can you wiggle your toes?" Maggie asked. She watched his feet. "I think I saw his big toe move, but I'm not sure. Did either of you see it?" She looked at David and Charlie.

"I might have," David said, but she could tell it was wishful thinking.

They could hear the ambulance in the distance, but she wasn't sure Brophy knew the siren sounded for him. "Everything's going to be okay. God sees you, Brophy, and He knows you're scared. He knows what *we* need." She looked at David and felt his concerned hand on her shoulder.

Brophy sniffled. "Why can't I move my legs?" Brophy tried to sit. "I wanna go home."

Maggie laid a tender yet firm hand on his chest. "Baby, Daddy would pick you up and carry you home if we thought that's what you needed, but you have to be a big boy and lie still. You're going to ride in an ambulance. What an adventure you'll have!" She created excitement with her voice while convincing herself not to fear. "I'll ride with you, okay?"

"Okay." His big eyes conveyed such trust, she almost moaned.

The siren's shrill approach made Maggie's skin crawl and the hair on her arms raise. "They're coming to help you, Brophy." She looked to David for comfort.

He held Brophy's hand. "The ambulance drivers will take good care of you."

Maggie nodded her head in agreement. "We can trust God. He knows what will happen next." *Even if we don't.*

The siren grew louder. How would she handle it if Brophy were paralyzed? She couldn't stand the thought. Her ninety-mile-a-minute, happy-go-lucky son in a wheelchair? Impossible!

"You're doing a good job of lying still." David's voice caught, a shadow of fear coloring his brow. "You're such a brave boy."

Charlie said, "When your daddy and I were little, we had a sledding accident."

"I'd forgotten about that," David said.

"I couldn't." Charlie stared across the pond at a distant memory. "Because it was my fault."

"That's right!" David slapped his knee, bringing Charlie's attention back to the present. "You finally admit it, you sorry louse."

"Focus, guys." Maggie had never heard this story. She continued to squat though her knees ached.

"Well, Brophy," Charlie said. "Your daddy couldn't move his legs either. But later on that night, he got all better."

"Me, too, Mommy?" Brophy looked at Maggie as if she knew the answer.

"Maybe." Maggie smoothed a wisp of hair away. She knelt down and kissed Brophy's cool forehead, praying it'd be so.

A frog croaked on the nearby bank, and a fish

jumped in the water. The abandoned fishing poles lay nearby. The ambulance drew closer, winding through her neighborhood. Her mind recorded every detail—sights and sounds magnified.

Brown winterized grass waved in the light breeze around them like a halo. Brophy suddenly reminded her of the babe in the manger. How had His mother felt, looking at Jesus, knowing He'd give His life for people like Maggie?

Maggie couldn't imagine allowing her son to die for anyone, especially not a stranger. She leaned close to shield Brophy. *Lord, protect my son. Please don't let him be paralyzed. He's too little to bear such a burden. And so am I.*

Brophy's teeth chattered.

She warmed his hands in hers. "Don't be scared, baby," she said, attempting to quell her own fear. Her insides quaked. She willed the tears begging for release to stay put.

She heard the thunder of footsteps approaching and stood to see Jill leading two emergency medical technicians, as well as Anne, Baxter, Blake, and Samantha.

The EMTs went to work, strapping Brophy to a backboard, asking questions, and recording information. She recognized one of them from church, a man everyone called Ace.

Brophy's eyes grew as wide as the brown pond to his left. "I've got to go pee-pee." He whined, "I can't hold it."

Maggie hovered over him. "You'll have to wait. You can't go until you get to the hospital and see the doctor."

Brophy tried to lift his upper body off the board. "I've got to go pee-pee. Now!"

Watching Brophy struggle wrought agony. Maggie kissed her finger and, scooting around the EMTs, she placed it on Brophy's cheek.

"Just go in your underwear," Ace told him. "It'll be all right."

Brophy looked scandalized. This contradicted his whole life and upbringing.

Maggie could picture Brophy running through the house bare-bottomed because he'd had an accident, yet here he was, refusing to wet his pants. Pride showed itself in unusual ways.

Speaking of bare-bottomed. She wondered if Ace had noticed the bathrobe hem, blown against her legs by the winter breeze. She felt her watermelon mask turn hot pink. Maggie put on her stern expression, so Brophy would know she meant business. "Just wet your pants, soldier boy. Daddy'll get you some more."

Brophy started shouting, "I want to go in the woods! Let me up!"

"I can't believe this." Maggie placed her hands on her hips and threatened, "Wet your pants and get it over with."

Brophy started wiggling, and his legs moved, commanding everyone's attention.

Maggie noticed Ace watching Brophy intently. "Is he supposed to move like that?" she asked.

Ace said, "Looks like he's getting some feeling back. I think it'd be all right if he went."

Maggie couldn't believe it. "You're not going to let him up before he sees the doctor! What if it's a spinal cord injury?" She stared at Ace, incredulous, her knuckles white on her coat.

Ace began releasing the restraints.

"I want another opinion." David laid a firm hand on his arm. "Please, Ace, take him to the hospital. He can wait."

"I can not." Brophy's little cheeks puffed out from the strain. "Look." Brophy wiggled his newly freed right ankle, demonstrating the feeling had returned. Then he wiggled his left as best he could within the constraints.

"I think it would be fine," the other EMT agreed, unstrapping his other leg.

"Honey," Maggie asked Brophy, "can you really feel your feet and legs?"

Brophy nodded. "Yup."

"Just like before you fell?"

Brophy stood and darted toward the bushes before anyone could stop him.

Ace said, "It was probably just a pinched nerve. That happens sometimes."

"Maybe that's what happened when we were kids." David shrugged. Charlie nodded.

Ace wasn't finished. "You combine that with the fear of everyone telling him not to move, and you can cause a little guy to believe he can't feel a thing—kinda like hearing Santa on Christmas Eve. You guys still want me to take him in? It's a pricey sleigh ride."

"Guess not, Ace." David clapped him on the back. He turned to shake the other EMT's hand. "Thanks for coming."

"A Merry Christmas miracle to you, folks." Ace wore a smile as jolly as Santa's. "And, Mrs. Mackenzie, you go get yourself some hot chocolate. You deserve some after this scare."

Her body shivered beneath the fake fur. Maggie's self-conscious nakedness made an appearance on her stained cheeks. Her left hand remained locked on the coat.

After Ace and his partner left, David popped Maggie's bottom. "I can't believe you came dressed like that." He swiped a drip of facial threatening her eyelid. "Humm. . .makes me remember a certain carefree girl I married once." He winked. "Oh, yeah. It was you, Maggie Mackenzie. I like you like this." He tweaked her nose.

Maggie let him smooth his robe's collar over her coat collar without protest. With David's arm around her and Brophy holding her hand, Maggie thanked God for her family. She hoped this close call would help keep their holidays in perspective, but she wasn't fooling herself. *It still won't be easy.*

Chapter 10

Maggie burst from several bubble baths without allowing the foam to fizzle before she learned to stay calm enough for a scented candle to burn down a quarter of an inch. It required robbing tiny bits of time from the family, but she'd accomplished the feat. Seven days after Brophy's accident, Maggie recorded her achievement in a newly purchased journal.

"What are you doing?" Samantha asked, finding Maggie in her new quiet spot. When Samantha lost her bedroom to Anne and started sleeping on the couch, Maggie had shoved a comfortable chair into the breakfast nook.

"Sitting, thinking, reading, and writing," Maggie answered without fretting. The Bible propped beneath the journal was open to Proverbs. She'd begun relying more heavily on Scripture for advice than the articles she'd clipped, but she hadn't found a bold dark line between the sacred and the secular as she'd expected. Truth, it'd turned out, showed up in unexpected places when she read God's Word daily. God reached Maggie in surprising ways when she stayed connected to Him in prayer.

"Why?" Samantha tilted her head. "Aren't you tempted to homeschool me or order me to do something?"

"A little bit," Maggie admitted. She took a sip of hazelnut coffee. "Do you want me to?"

"Whoa. Mom, this is weird. This has been going on for a week now. You sure you don't want to teach me something?"

"Yes, but all lessons aren't in a textbook." Maggie replaced the china cup on the saucer and moved her journal aside. She flipped a page in the Bible.

Samantha moved across the kitchen, opened the cabinet, and grabbed a handful of Fruit Loops cereal. "Where's Brophy? Do I need to watch him?"

"Blake and Baxter are keeping him busy, but it'd be great if you checked on them now and then." Maggie glanced down and read, *"A kindhearted woman gains respect."*

Samantha popped the cereal into her mouth, one

colorful loop at a time. "You mean we're on break?"

"I am." Maggie looked up and stifled a smile.

Samantha frowned. "Then. . .I am. . .too?" She sounded uncertain.

"If you like." Maggie resumed reading.

"Okay. So what are we doing today?"

Maggie smiled at her daughter. "I don't know. What are *you* doing?"

"Mom, come on. This is weird. It's like you've quit or something."

Maggie stretched. "Just taking a break to figure some things out."

"But the house isn't decorated yet, and Christmas is around the corner."

Maggie understood her daughter's tension but chose not to worry. "Feel free." Maggie fanned out a hand.

"Fine. I'm going to the pasture to look for some holly. The mantel's bare."

"Great." Maggie watched Samantha put on her coat and leave just as David rounded the corner.

"Where's she going?" David leaned down for a morning hug.

"To gather holly, wonder of wonders." Maggie couldn't believe she hadn't begged or bribed Samantha to help.

"What's for breakfast, Mags?" David had the day

off, and she usually cooked something special.

"Whatever you want."

He ruffled her hair. "So, you're feeling more like yourself. I'm glad."

"Better than ever." Maggie couldn't believe how taking an intermission had settled her. She felt more prayerful. Stepping off the holiday treadmill hadn't hurt the family ecosystem. Anne had done the dinner dishes twice. Jill played with the kids and encouraged Maggie to relax. Pop's gallbladder hadn't acted up all week. Maggie suspected it might have something to do with the reduced stress around the house. Ma even seemed calm, her dementia less noticeable.

"I'll take two eggs over easy," David interrupted her reverie. The environmental changes hadn't improved his manners.

"The kitchen's in there." She pointed as though he were clueless.

David bristled. "Come on, Maggie. This is getting ridiculous. You're not doing anything you usually do. Do you need counseling?"

That hurt. She searched the Bible as if she'd lost her place. The pages blurred. *Did* she need a counselor? "Maybe."

"Our insurance covers it."

"Fine."

"Perhaps you're depressed."

She looked at him in horror. She bit her lip and shrugged. "Maybe I'm just changing."

"Why would you want to? You're perfect."

Maggie volleyed the question. "Why wouldn't I want to change?"

"I'm worried about you, Maggie. You're not yourself." He flicked a business card into her lap. "I made an appointment for you two weeks from Tuesday. Four o'clock. Promise you'll go?"

She looked at the psychologist's card. Maybe a shrink *could* explain how she felt. "Okay." She felt like a child.

"About those eggs. . ." David waited.

She couldn't believe he had signed her up for counseling. "Make them yourself, honey."

Chapter 11

Maggie stayed up half the night composing her speech, gathering thoughts from her previously drafted, yet unsent, letter. She hoped to end this before seeing the psychologist. But now, as she stood before her puzzled family, she thought she might need mental help if she confronted them.

Perhaps she should wait. Not invite trouble. Postpone the changes until next year. Hadn't they been through enough with the transformation she'd already accomplished? She silently recited the quote she'd taped to the bathroom mirror: *If this were easy, I would have done it long ago.* But she still couldn't find the courage to speak.

A twin twitched on each of Anne's knees. Pop and Ma Mackenzie claimed two recliners. Ma snored. Pop rocked. Samantha flopped onto her stomach, elbows bent. Beside her, David embraced their wiggly son. Jill stood next to Charlie, who drummed his fingers on the mantel.

Maggie swallowed what felt like a hard-boiled egg. She cleared her throat. "This Christmas we're going to. . ."

If this were a Hallmark commercial, everything would turn out fine and there'd be greeting-card emotions to commemorate the ending. *Wishful thinking.*

Maggie started over, "You know how frustrated I got this Thanksgiving? It wore me to the wishbone. Well, I don't want to be selfish at Christmas. I'm willing to share the fatigue and cooking chores." A high, nervous giggle erupted, but no one joined her.

She'd hoped to amuse them, not make herself sound like a hysterical martyr. Their awkward silence should have stifled her, but it made her laugh instead. She felt like an idiot. Her shoulders shook. Her nose ran. She hated being this nervous. *David already thinks I'm crazy. Now I'm confirming it.*

She forced herself to begin with him. "David, I'm taking you up on your Cajun-fried turkey. You and Pop can oversee the bird." Her voice raised an octave. Someone would think she'd consumed helium.

Pop said, "I can snap some beans. I know how to boil water." He'd caught on.

Maggie bit her lip. She preferred the green bean

casserole seasoned with mushroom soup and Velveeta cheese to the boiled kind. "Uh. . .thanks, but the green beans go to Samantha." Maggie looked at her daughter. "I'll show you how. It's easy." Maggie felt her way forward. "Jill, how 'bout if you take the sweet potatoes, and Charlie, the pecan pie?"

They agreed.

"Anne, if you'll take the pump. . ."

"I hate that we repeat Thanksgiving. It's the same meal twice in a row." Samantha wrinkled her nose. "Can't we have something different for Christmas?"

Maggie thought a moment. "I guess so." She'd never thought of it.

David stood. "If we're going to implement change, dear, we might as well really shake things up."

Maggie preferred control. "It's tradition. I use Ma's old recipes. Actually, they were her mother's." She glanced at Ma, asleep with her mouth agape.

Anne looked at Ma, too. "She'll never know. I have a great recipe for summer squash with Rotel tomatoes. It'll go perfect with the Cajun turkey."

"Okay." Maggie smiled, thankful for Anne's input. "Let's still do pumpkin pie."

"I'd prefer apple," Anne said.

Maggie frowned. "Christmas without pumpkin pie?"

"Sounds good to me," David said.

Charlie came to Maggie's rescue. "I'll make the pumpkin, or would everyone rather have pecan?"

"With my cholesterol, pumpkin's better for me," Pop said.

"Pumpkin it is. Who's going to buy the groceries?" Charlie asked.

"Let's see." Maggie hadn't thought of that. She looked at her mixed-up list. "So far we have Cajun-fried turkey."

"So much for my cholesterol," Pop said.

Maggie rolled her eyes. "We have the green bean casserole. . . ."

"I hate those green beans." Samantha put one hand on her hip. "And I don't want fried turkey either." She frowned.

Pop leaned forward. "I'm not sure I can eat anything spicy, dear. Cajun turkey and Rotel squash sound like invitations to the emergency room. Though I'm sure your squash is real tasty, Anne." He smiled apologetically.

Maggie thought he should apologize to her. She scratched out the squash, then reconsidered. "Make it with less spice, Anne; then Pop can handle it. We need another vegetable if we eliminate the beans."

Ma stirred and opened her eyes. "Rots," she said.

"Rots?" Maggie asked.

"She's trying to say carrots," Pop explained.

Ma stuck out her tongue and licked her lips.

Maggie offered an encouraging smile to her mother-in-law. "I'm not sure it'd be Christmas without carrots or green bean casserole."

"How 'bout mashed potatoes? I wondered why we didn't have 'em with the dressing. Grandma always did," Charlie said.

"Yes. What about the dressing?" Anne asked.

"It's up for grabs," Maggie said, trying to distance herself.

"What are you making?" Samantha asked Maggie.

All eyes fell on her. Maggie swallowed another boiled egg. "I'm on cleanup crew. And I promise I won't put the dishes outside." She winked at Jill. "Other than that, you're on your own."

"How come you're getting outta cooking?" Samantha asked.

"It's somebody else's turn. Now, who will take the dressing?"

"No one makes it like you do," Pop prodded her with guilt.

"How do we know?" Maggie tapped her list with the pencil eraser. She watched it bounce without making eye contact with the family. "Jill, you want to tackle it?"

"If Charlie'll help, I'll try, but I'm not promising much. I'm no chef."

"Charlie?" Maggie looked at her brother-in-law.

"Gee-whiz! I got married so someone else would cook."

Jill chucked a pillow at him. "You married the wrong girl, buddy. Maggie told me you know how to cook. Your secret's out."

"A real manly man." David thumped his brother on the back.

Charlie burped, then sniggered with David.

Maggie ignored them. "I forgot you, Pop."

"I wondered. I can do more than watch David raise my cholesterol with his fried-up turkey." He sounded hurt.

Maggie checked her list. "Oversee the rolls. They'll need heating."

Pop looked at his daughter-in-law with concern. "Maggie, honey, have you not felt appreciated? Did we hurt your feelings?"

"You compliment me, Pop. You all do, but nobody helps."

David said, "You have impossibly high standards, Maggie. Admit it."

Maggie felt her throat constrict. "So? I want everything right. What's wrong with that?"

"You want everything *perfect.*" David stood and draped an arm around her shoulders. "You sure you're ready to give up the perfect Christmas?"

Chapter 12

"Charlie can't sleep," Jill told Maggie the following week. She rubbed her eyes. "The bed's too soft and it's getting worse. He kept me up half the night with back spasms. I'm not sure what we're going to do." She reached for the coffeepot.

Maggie sponged the kitchen sink. *A hotel comes to mind.* She moved to the den couch and folded her legs Indian-style.

Jill took the chair across from her, Santa mug in hand. She pulled her leg up and wrapped an arm around one knee. "Ma wouldn't know what to do in a new bed. . . . Maybe Anne and the boys could move. . . ." She massaged her temples with her free hand. "Does this couch fold out? Oh, that's right. Samantha's using it."

Maggie didn't want to think what the children might learn if the newlyweds moved to the den. "Our

mattress is firm. I guess you could give our bed a try."
You'd give your life away if someone needed it, Maggie.

David would disapprove. But maybe he'd remember what it felt like to be "in love." *If only!*

Jill's eyes blinked with hope. "Are you sure?" She held the steaming coffee mug to her forehead, closed her eyes, and sighed. "You give so much. I didn't want to ask."

"Let Charlie try it tonight and see if it helps. Then we'll decide." She'd tell David it was a temporary arrangement, though she doubted it. They had the most comfortable bed in the house.

Jill stood. "I'll take care of the sheets. You're great, Maggie. I owe you."

Big-time. "It's no problem." Maggie presented an article she'd clipped. "I thought we could make these cute ornaments with the kids today. Keep 'em busy awhile." *And get my mind off moving out of my own room.*

Jill looked at the photos of the tri-bead and candy cane ornaments. "I like today's 'de-stressing' plan."

"One a day—like vitamins." Maggie tried to stand, but her foot cramped. "Ouch." Maggie rubbed her aching instep, then her heel.

"Do your feet hurt?"

"Sometimes."

"I have the best cure for aching feet." Jill went to the

kitchen cabinet where Maggie stored the pans. "Is this the biggest pot you have?" She indicated the stockpot.

"Yes, why?"

"You ask too many questions. Keep reading. I'll be right back."

Wanting to show Jill a good example of Christian living, Maggie opened her Bible. Her eyes roved down the page. *"Do not fret—it leads only to evil." Everywhere I turn, God sends the same message—don't worry.*

"Close your eyes." Jill inserted a pillow behind Maggie's neck, then tapped her forehead. "Lean back."

Maggie heard water running in the sink. She peeked.

Jill lifted a filled pot, sprinkled in something granular that sounded like rock salt, then swished it around with her hand. She tucked a hand towel under one arm, picked up the heavy pot, and walked toward Maggie. "No peeking."

Maggie shut her eyes. She felt the soft towel go under her bare feet, felt Jill lift her pant's leg, and guide her tired feet into hot water. She caught a whiff of peppermint. The water tingled against her skin.

Maggie curled her toes so they'd fit in the pot. The water rose ankle-height. Some splashed over the edge. "Why the princess treatment? You're the one who didn't sleep. I should be doing this for you." She eyed Jill. "This feels incredible." She stretched her toes.

"I wanted to do something nice for you. When you mentioned the candy cane ornaments, I thought of a peppermint footbath. Isn't it relaxing?" Jill tuned the radio to a Christmas station. She pulled one of Maggie's feet from the minty water. Jill massaged the tightness away. First the toes, then the foot, up to the ankle, and finally the calf.

"Oh, my goodness. This is wonderful. I can't believe you'd do this for me."

Jill sat back on her knees. "I can't believe you'd give up your bed. What're you reading?"

"Psalms." Maggie hadn't thought Jill would ask.

"I thought maybe you were reading the Christmas story." Jill glanced at the manger scene. "Read it to me?"

"Silent Night" played in the background as Maggie turned to Luke, chapter 2. She practically had to quote from memory because tears blocked her view.

Jill tenderly dried Maggie's feet and legs, then rubbed in lotion. "I love that story."

Before Maggie could steady her pounding heart enough to explain how Jill's actions had mirrored Christ's love, Jill said, "Let's tackle those ornaments. Where're the kids?"

"The twins and Brophy are outside. And Samantha's around here somewhere. I thought Ma could make the tri-bead wreaths with the boys; they're so easy. The rest of us can make the peppermint hearts. This way we can decorate the tree without unpacking any more boxes." She grinned.

"Aha! Ulterior motive." Jill poured the footbath into the sink while Maggie found the glue gun. "Show me first how to melt the white chocolate; then you round up the family," Jill said.

Snap. Another peppermint stick fractured, frustrating the perfectionist in Maggie. "The article didn't say it'd be hard to unwrap these." Maggie surveyed the split canes. "You can't make hearts with pieces."

"Let's make whatever shapes we can using the broken ones and hearts from the ones that don't break." Jill glued candy cane pieces together, creating a snowflake.

"The melted chocolate will hold the hearts together, even if they're broken." Anne poured white chocolate into the center of two canes facing each other on waxed paper, and decorated the surface with crushed peppermint.

"That looks just like the article." Jill unwrapped a cane with success.

Maggie bent more pipe cleaners at the end, so Ma and the boys could continue their tri-bead project. "Remember, red, then white. Red, then white."

Bing Crosby crooned "White Christmas."

Brophy slid his hand up the pipe cleaner with force, sending little beads spewing across the table toward Blake. Brophy pointed. "He took my beads." He looked like he couldn't figure out how Blake got his beads. "He took my beads," he repeated, frustrated.

"You knocked your own beads off," Blake said with seven-year-old superiority.

"Blake didn't take your beads," Samantha explained, placing Brophy on her lap. "Here, help me make a chocolate heart." She offered an unwrapped cane to Brophy. When he tucked it in his mouth, she didn't complain.

Maggie noticed Samantha's attitude had changed toward her little brother, and she attributed it to the accident at the pond. *Thank You, God, for peace in my family.*

That afternoon they baked and decorated homemade sugar cookies for the neighbors. In the evening, David and Charlie took them all caroling and "cookie-ing," as Maggie liked to call it. They drove around the neighborhood in the back of a pickup truck, singing and taking turns distributing cookies. Even Anne had fun, and it seemed some of her worry had lifted.

After David and the family went to bed, Maggie

stayed up to read the story of Jesus washing his disciples' feet. Not wanting to disturb Samantha, she dimmed the lights and curled into her cozy chair.

Maggie considered her new sister-in-law. It was Jill's gentle acceptance of her that allowed Maggie to discover something likable inside herself. Maggie didn't feel the need to be perfect with Jill around. The Bible said Christ showed His friends "the full extent of his love" by washing their feet. Jesus said, "I have set you an example that you should do as I have done for you." Did Jill realize the significance of her gift?

Christ had washed Judas's feet, too—the one who in a matter of hours betrayed Him, leading to His death on the cross. How could Christ accept someone who would betray Him? *Someone like me.*

Tears welled in her eyes and slid down her cheeks. She was Judas. She was the overworked Martha. She was the believer who worried and fretted her way through life. Not just at Christmastime. And Christ. Who was He to her? She pictured Him washing her feet as tenderly as Jill had. She slipped off her fuzzy slippers as if her feet rested on holy ground. He'd done it for her today. Through Jill.

Maggie dropped her head. She clasped her hands over her heart. God didn't need her to be perfect. He accepted her. When she acted like Judas and betrayed

Him. Or, like Martha, failed to recognize Him. And now, like Mary, as she worshiped Him! Christ accepted her as she was!

Oh, come let us adore Him. The familiar hymn matched her heart's song.

Jesus didn't love her any more or any less because of her failings. Suddenly, His love felt deep and wide, broader than she'd ever imagined. Jesus had delivered Christmas to her doorstep. Like a baby's gentle coo, it had awakened her slumbering blindness. A deep bubbling laughter welled up inside, a heartfelt joy and freedom she'd rarely experienced before.

"Mom?" Samantha called from the adjoining den, having awakened to Maggie's mirth.

"I'm fine." Maggie quieted her joy. "Go back to sleep." She leaned her head back, intending to pray, but dropped off to sleep instead.

Maggie awoke around 2:00 a.m., dazed and disoriented. She rubbed the stiffness from her neck, unplugged the tree, and performed a routine check of locks and lights. She turned left into her bedroom, entered the bathroom, and closed the door so as not to wake David.

She washed her face, brushed her teeth, and put on her pajamas. Flipping the light switch off, she made her way to the bed, avoiding the chair that had relentlessly stubbed her toe on many occasions.

Maggie pulled back the comforter and slid between the cool sheets. She rolled toward David and threw her arm around his middle.

A female scream pierced her eardrums.

Maggie rolled off the bed's edge onto the floor.

"Holy smoke!" a male voice yelled, confusing her even more. It didn't belong to David.

Maggie squealed, trying to make sense of the situation.

The male voice in bed moaned. "Ack! Ouch. Ouch. My back," he said.

The woman giggled.

The voices finally registered as Charlie's and Jill's.

David burst into the room. "What's going on in here?" He switched on the lights, bathing his nearly naked brother and sister-in-law in brightness.

The newlyweds fought for cover beneath the tangled sheets. "Cut the lights!" Charlie yelled.

A bomb of nervous relief and gut-wrenching hilarity exploded in the room. Pop ran in, armed with a fire extinguisher. And before they could stop him, he doused them all.

Ma held a flashlight backward, illuminating her flannel gown. She shouted without a hint of dementia, "Someone yelled fire! Someone yelled fire!"

Maggie sounded like an inexperienced trombone

102

player, spewing laughter through her pinched lips. She collapsed on the bed next to Jill.

"Ow." Charlie slid from the bed, claiming the sheet. Jill grabbed the comforter in hysterics.

Charlie danced a crippled jig. "My back. Gee-whiz! Have some respect next time, Maggie. Holy smoke!"

"That's what you heard, Pop," Maggie managed to say between giggles. "Charlie yelled smoke, not fire."

Chapter 13

Anne knocked on Brophy's door early the next morning with the leopard-print traveling tote over her shoulder. "Maggie, I'm going home."

Maggie sat up in bed. "Why? We were finally starting to have some fun." She grabbed her robe and belted it as they moved toward the kitchen.

Anne's suitcases waited beside the door. "I talked to John last night. All the fun we've been having around here, and Brophy's accident last week, well. . .I've seen what's missing in our family." Anne dashed away the sadness. "John's not so bad. . .oh, he can be difficult, but so can David. I've seen that. I thought you had the perfect marriage."

Maggie stopped and faced her. "Me? You've *got* to be kidding." She snickered. "I thought *you* did."

"Clearly, we need to spend more time together."

As they neared Samantha, asleep on the couch, Maggie lowered her voice, "Want some hot chocolate?"

"Like we used to? Sure."

Many sister secrets had been shared over mugs of steaming cocoa. Maggie put the water on to boil. She removed a canister of homemade hot chocolate mix and a bag of mini marshmallows from the cabinet.

"John wants me to bring the boys home. He says he's going to take some time off."

Maggie turned toward Anne. "Will you come back for Christmas?" She set two Christmas mugs on the counter.

"I don't think so. We need time alone. Baxter and Blake hardly know their dad."

Maggie couldn't say the same for David's relationship with her children. "I know what you mean about needing time with your husband. I hope everything will be all right between you and John. I've been praying for you." Maggie laid a hand on Anne's arm.

Tears leapt to Anne's lashes. She blinked. "I have to believe it's going to be. That's why I'm going home. I was running when I came here. Now I'm ready to face the hard stuff. Thanks, Maggie."

"For what?"

"For showing me life can swirl around you, and you don't have to cave in. You stay sane in craziness."

"I'm not so sure I'm sane." Maggie thought of the counselor David wanted her to see.

"Oh, you are. You might be a pushover with a big heart, but you haven't lost your ability to connect with people around you."

Maggie frowned, trying to sort the compliment from the way it made her feel. *Pushover* wasn't her favorite trait.

"You know what I mean. You want to please people so much that you ignore your own needs. Jill and I talked about it."

Maggie scrubbed chocolate powder from the countertop, uncomfortable knowing she'd been the topic of their conversation.

"I've been watching how you take care of everyone. Noticing how generous you are. To a fault."

Maggie felt her eyebrows rise. Was Anne complimenting her or being critical?

"Then when I saw you run out the door, looking such a fright, unafraid to meet the challenge ahead no matter how you looked or what else you had to do—I got the cookies out of the oven, by the way. Well. . .I felt small and shallow. No matter who was hurt, I wouldn't have run from the house half-naked with that goop smeared all over my face, not even for my boys or John. I would have thought of myself, my needs, my image.

I would have been wearing a carefully applied mask—one that says everything's okay—not a drippy facial, daring the world to see me come undone. I want to be a mom and wife like you."

Like me? Maggie stood a little taller.

"Mom and Dad would have been proud. You behave more like an older sister than I do. You've made a good life for yourself, Magpie." Anne used her pet childhood name.

"I don't know what to say." She looked at Anne—her flawless skin, hair, and makeup. Her perfect life wasn't flawless beneath the surface.

Anne interrupted Maggie's thoughts. "Tell me you love me, and you'll pray for me as I go. The challenges back home won't be easy to fix."

Maggie opened the canister of mix. "Is there any way I can help?"

Anne smiled. "Yes."

"How?" Maggie spooned hot chocolate mix into Anne's mug, then hers.

"By continuing to find ways to pamper and care for yourself. I like my less-stressed little sis." She offered Maggie a hug.

Maggie welcomed the hug, glad for sister-love.

"I'll call you later when you're not so overwhelmed."

Maggie rolled her eyes. "And when might that be?"

She poured hot water over the chocolate and stirred.

"Sooner than you might think," Jill said as she entered the room with Charlie right behind her. "We're going apartment hunting."

Charlie put his arms around Jill's waist and leaned his chin on her head. "Don't worry. We'll move back in February." He winked at Anne.

Maggie's eyebrows arched in surprise. *Why?* The question formed in her mind but never reached her lips because life distracted her. She reached for two more mugs, scooped in cocoa and water, then stirred. Maggie topped the four mugs with marshmallows.

Anne accepted a reindeer mug from Maggie. "You know Ma will need a nursing home soon."

"I couldn't do that to her." Maggie offered a Santa mug to Jill and an elf mug to Charlie.

Jill blew on the top of her chocolate to cool it. "You might not have to. Charlie and David have been talking to Pop about retirement centers."

As usual, God had a plan. "David and I need some time alone. Actually, I've been thinking we need to get away." Maggie's deepest need lay bare and exposed.

"Such a perfect lead-in." Anne held her mug in both hands and took a careful sip. "Charlie, go get David and Pop."

"Lead-in to what?" Maggie asked.

Jill stirred more of the extra-rich chocolate into her mug. "You'll see. Just remember, I told you you'd love your Christmas present." She popped a marshmallow into her mouth.

While Charlie went to wake David, Anne reached into her leopard-print tote and withdrew an envelope. She set it on the counter.

Maggie eyed it as she put more water on to boil. "I can't imagine what that is. Is it for me?"

Neither woman answered.

"You knew about this?" Maggie asked Jill.

Jill nodded. "Anne and I talked about it at Thanksgiving. I thought we'd have to wait till Christmas; then Anne pulled us aside last night and said we should do it today." Her eyes crinkled with delight.

David, Pop, and Charlie walked in.

"Drum roll, please," Anne said.

Charlie tapped a cadence of beats on the counter.

"Maggie. David." Anne acted as master of ceremonies. "This is for you two." She presented the envelope like an Oscar.

David sniffed it, held it up to the light, and shook it.

"Open it, silly." Maggie punched his arm. "Don't keep me in suspense any longer."

David looked at his brother. "I don't know if we can afford to open it, Mags. It might be a gag gift. Charlie, did you have anything to do with this? There aren't any snakes in here that'll jump out at me, are there?"

Charlie gave a wry smile. "Maybe."

"No way. I don't trust him." David laid it on the counter.

Maggie grabbed the envelope and tore the seal. "I don't care what you say."

"A truer word was never spoken," David shot back.

Everyone laughed at the couple's banter.

After giving Maggie and David a chance to review the information inside, Anne said, "They're reservations to John's and my time-share lodge. It comes available in February. By then your schedule should be less crazy."

Maggie looked into Anne's sparkling eyes. "You're the best sister in the world. How can we ever thank you?" Maggie hugged Anne close and whispered, "Are you sure about this? If you and John have issues to tackle, don't you need this vacation more than we do?"

Anne whispered back, "No. That's what we need to work on—how to become a family like you. Appreciating each other won't come from getting away from the boys; for us it will happen by staying home."

Anne pulled back and announced, "John plans to take the rest of December off—until the boys go back to school. Maggie's shown me how important family is."

Amazement spread across Maggie's face. Her eyes

widened. "In all this craziness? With me throwing the meal back in everyone's face—and staging my own sit-in? No way."

"Yes, way!" Anne said. "Grabbing for sanity in the middle of an overworked holiday is acceptable, little sis. I could tell you set your boundaries with God's help. I felt proud when you *finally* stood up for yourself. But since doing less is rarely an option with you. . ." Anne indicated with her hand that Jill should take the next part.

"Yes." Jill repeated, "Since doing less is rarely an option for you, Maggie, we wanted to give you something more to do—pack for a ski trip. And you don't have to look at a magazine to enjoy this kink in your schedule."

Anne smiled her biggest. "Skiing is perfectly self-indulgent. And the lodge is *so* romantic."

David wrapped an arm around Maggie's waist.

Jill opened the drawer and handed Maggie another envelope.

"Where'd that come from?"

"Oh, we keep our secrets well hidden." Jill sipped her chocolate.

Maggie opened the envelope.

Jill said in childlike excitement, "We put enough money in here to foot the bill for eating out all week, and Charlie and I threw in a couple's massage package I found online. You're going to join the facial sisterhood, David."

"Fat chance," he said.

"Y'all are incredible," Maggie said. She swallowed hard. "You've given me a gift I didn't deserve and couldn't afford."

"Kinda like our Savior," Jill said to Maggie's amazement. "It's beginning to feel a lot like Christmas around here."

After Anne and the boys left for the airport with Charlie and Jill, David said, "Samantha's on the phone. Let's go see if we still have a bedroom of our own."

They sat on the bed with the tousled sheets left by the honeymooners. For some reason, the mess didn't bother Maggie. She snuggled into David's embrace considering the gift, not expecting another one.

David spoke into her hair, "I thought you might like to finish decorating the tree tonight, with just our family. I'll get the rest of the boxes from the attic and send the lovers out with Ma and Pop." David took her hand. "I miss family time."

She stroked her favorite sheets. "I miss our bed."

"Charlie and I are going apartment hunting today.

I think you scared the wits out of them last night."

They shared a hearty laugh. David took her hand and stroked her knuckles. "I'm sorry I haven't been much help lately."

She snickered. "When have you *ever* been a big help, sir?"

"I'm trying to apologize here, Mags." He removed his arm from her shoulder and cupped his hands in his lap.

She sobered, anticipating an oft-ignored apology.

He bit his lip and looked toward the ceiling.

She gave him time.

"I didn't realize how you felt until Thanksgiving. But I didn't pay attention until you called the family meeting. Then after Brophy's accident. . ." He swallowed hard. "God's been dealing with me, Mags."

She knew he meant it. "Anne mentioned the accident."

"You wearing my bathrobe was a turn-on, in case you didn't know." His eyes crinkled playfully.

He couldn't stay serious, but that was okay. Maggie felt herself go warm inside. She burrowed her hand in his. Apologies by David were so rare she gravitated toward humor, as well. "You're just suffering from holiday celibacy." She touched his hair with her fingertips. Sleeping with Brophy had more disadvantages than elbows in the cheek.

"Another reason for Jill and Charlie to get out." He patted the mattress.

"Amen." She let him pull her downward despite the unmade bed. His shoulder formed a pillow.

He cupped her chin like she was the dearest, most precious woman in the world. "At Thanksgiving, I wanted life to go on as it always had. And I was mad at you. But watching you last week, I knew I needed to adjust, or you'd break."

He kissed her neck. "I rode you pretty hard about all the changes you were making."

"Uh-huh." She relished the answer to her prayers.

"I don't like change, Maggie, but I realized something incredible. You're *not* the one changing. Not really."

She leaned up on one elbow to see what he meant. "You'd better explain that one."

"You are more like the girl I married now—relaxed, playful, happy." He enfolded her with his arms.

Her cheek found a resting place near his heart.

He rubbed her shoulder in rhythmic circles. "You're self-sufficient. You're beautiful."

Her heart leapt. *He thinks I'm beautiful.*

"You're Christ-centered, Maggie—more now than ever."

Wow! She couldn't believe what she was hearing.

David wasn't finished. "You take care of a jillion

things at once, yet stay focused and determined. You *are* the girl I married. You never were a pushover, Mags." He kissed the top of her head.

Maggie cocked her head, considering. Something didn't make sense. "But what about the counselor you said I needed?"

He rubbed her shoulder. "I canceled the appointment."

Maggie kept her eyes on him. She didn't understand.

His lip twitched, a sure sign of discomfort. "Charlie said *I* needed to go. Said *you* had your life under control. Maybe he's right, but I'd feel more comfortable if you went with me."

"We both have things to work on," she offered. "We could go to marriage counseling if you think it would help." She didn't know how he'd respond.

He looked embarrassed as he gazed toward the ceiling. "I want to become the man you should've married, Maggie." Their eyes met in an intimate exchange. "One who'll make things easier on you around here, not harder. You don't deserve how childish I am sometimes." He reached for her left hand and fingered her wedding band.

Maggie studied the man she'd fallen in love with so long ago.

He gave a sheepish grin. "Maggie Mackenzie, you didn't know it when you resigned at Thanksgiving, but you set some powerful changes in motion. You showed us that while 'it's more blessed to give than receive,' it works best when everyone shares the giving. When you slammed the door on the familiar, you forced us all to find another way. A better way."

Maggie chuckled inside. *Now that's something worth giving thanks for.*

PAMELA DOWD lives in east Texas with her husband, Rodney. They have three daughters and one son-in-law. Pamela enjoys creating strong stories with characters who display candid, growing relationships with God. She has published short stories, devotionals, magazine articles, and greeting cards, including her own line, Cookie Jar Greetings, published by Warner Press. Besides writing, Pamela has been a private school principal, a pre-school director, a kindergarten teacher, a legal secretary, and a children's clothing designer. On street or treadmill she enjoys reading and walking simultaneously! Pamela loves to hear from her readers. E-mail: grammargurl@hotmail.com.

My True Love Gave to Me. . .

by Christine Lynxwiler

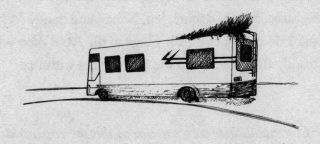

Dedication

To *my* favorite author, Tracey Bateman, who took time to read this for me every time I revised, even though she was on a killer deadline. I couldn't have made it without you cheering me on, Trace. There's never been a truer friend.

To Kevin, for always helping me find my way home when I'm lost in the dark.

And finally, to everyone who reaches out to others, whether through an organized volunteer program or individually. You're an inspiration to me.

Special thanks and appreciation to: Lynette, Jan, Pam, Susie, Susan, Rachel, Jen, Nancy, and Sandy. What would I do without you all? Hugs to the ACRWers who so readily shared their RVing experiences with me!

*"Command those who are rich in this present world
not to be arrogant nor to put their hope in wealth,
which is so uncertain, but to put their hope in God,
who richly provides us with everything for our enjoyment.
Command them to do good, to be rich in good deeds,
and to be generous and willing to share."*
1 Timothy 6:17–18

Chapter 1

...The Key to a Borrowed RV

I gritted my teeth and shifted the cardboard box against the spindly pull-down attic ladder. Whoever invented these contraptions obviously hadn't considered that people would be going up and down the narrow steps with their arms full.

Of course, I could be transferring my aggravation to some nameless inventor instead of placing the blame where it belonged—squarely on the shoulders of my beloved husband with his recent mysterious attitude.

"The—" I pressed the side of my face against the cardboard, clutching my burden tightly, in spite of the dust particles crawling up my nose. "—very—" I lowered one foot, tapping air until I found the next step. It would be a disaster to fall with this box. "—idea!" I jumped off the last step and landed with a thud, gripping my priceless cargo.

For sixteen years, Thanksgiving afternoon at the Lassiters had meant one thing—putting up the Christmas tree.

I set the old box carefully on the hardwood floor in the den and stared at the words I'd written the year Phillip and I had married—*Fragile: Christmas Ornaments*. On the corner of the box, where I always denoted our storage containers with such titles as *Summer* or *Winter* or *Open When Amanda Turns Ten*, I had printed *Thanksgiving Day*. Even then, at the ripe old age of twenty, I never left anything to chance. Spell it out. No beating around the bush.

No doubt about it; today was the day.

So why had my husband, who loved Christmas as much as I did, announced cryptically at breakfast that instead of putting up the tree this afternoon he had something else planned? Granted, he'd been acting strange for at least a week, but his proclamation had thrown my whole day off-kilter. And then he'd driven off after lunch to take his parents home without another word about it.

"Mom, I can't find today's paper!" The yell from the living room settled my pounding heart some. The kids obviously hadn't paid much attention to their dad's announcement. This very minute fourteen-year-old Amanda and twelve-year-old Seth were scouring the house for catalogs, sales flyers, and every merchandising media they could get their hands on.

I have my traditions. . .they have theirs. While Phillip and I wrangle with the tree, they make long Christmas wish lists.

I smiled, remembering how those lists evolved from a four-year-old's childishly scrawled T-R-U-C-K or D-O-L-L to a certain brand-name DVD/VCR player—right down to the model number, the store that had it on sale, and what day the sale ended. When it came to Christmas, my children were like me. They left nothing to chance.

I grabbed a fluffy towel from the bathroom to lay the ornaments on while I arranged them for hanging. Phillip always laughed at my ceremonious "spreading of the towel." A twinge of guilt shot through me. *Maybe I should wait and see what he has to say when he gets home.*

No, if I forged ahead and got a jump-start on things, then hopefully whatever Phillip had in mind wouldn't take long. We'd be back on schedule by supper. Never let it be said that Penny Lassiter couldn't compromise.

I settled on my knees and reverently opened the flaps of the box. The slightly musty smell wafted up to me like a comfortable old friend.

Each ornament, wrapped in tissue paper, nestled into its own little section of the eggcrate cardboard dividers I'd long ago modified for this purpose. Just as it did every year on this day, anticipation fluttered in my stomach. My excitement pushed away any lingering doubts about Phillip's strange behavior.

I carefully lifted the first treasure, unwrapped the tissue, and stared at the brittle gingerbread man. A childhood memory leaped into my mind, replaying in video-clip fashion. I ran my finger along the word "Penny" roughly engraved on the tummy above the date.

What a shock it had been to see this homemade clay ornament instead of the collectible one my parents normally bought for my sisters and me. An uneasy feeling had crept into my ten-year-old heart that day, and my mom's pleading smile confirmed that the gingerbread man was a precursor of things to come.

That same uneasy feeling, only slightly more grownup, had visited me again six weeks ago when Phillip came home with news of his company downsizing. He'd been let go. I didn't doubt he'd find another job. He's a wonderful accountant. But one of the first things I thought of was that if it didn't happen soon, we'd have no money for Christmas.

As he'd checked out the want ads, I'd remembered the year I was ten. There'd been a bad drought, and my parents had almost lost the farm. Of course, I didn't realize that then. All I knew was that I received a homemade ornament instead of the normal store-bought kind, a hand-knitted hat, scarf, and matching gloves instead of the hoped-for alarm clock radio. The new bicycle I'd wanted looked suspiciously like my sister's old one, only with fresh red paint. My sisters hadn't fared any better.

With Phillip's termination notice clutched in my hand, I couldn't keep from fretting. In spite of my best intentions, for the first time in their lives, would our kids have a disappointing Christmas? And, horror of horrors, would I have to learn to knit?

Thankfully, God worked it out. Phillip ended up with a six-month severance pay package, and before his thirty days' notice was up a few days ago, he'd secured an even better job with a new company. Instead of learning to knit, I'd been able to start my shopping early. Then came the most wonderful news of all—Phillip wouldn't begin the new position until January. I'd have him around every day to help make this Christmas the best ever.

Shaking the unhappy might-have-beens from

my mind, I removed the tissue paper from the next ornament. A small crystal heart with an etching of a couple in a horse-drawn sleigh proclaimed *Our First Christmas Together*. I held it up to the light. We'd married December 19, and Phillip had given this to me on our honeymoon. We'd just been two crazy kids in love. Ever since that day, this had been my favorite ornament.

"Penny! What are you doing?"

I jerked at the sound of Phillip's voice, and the heart slipped from my fingers. I lunged to catch it. For an agonizing second, my fingertip touched the slick surface, but my hands came together grasping air. The most precious ornament I owned crashed to the hardwood floor and shattered into pieces.

"Oh, no." Phillip rushed over and knelt beside me. "Honey, I'm so sorry." He put his arm around my shoulders, but I didn't move.

I stared at the tiny crystal slivers and blinked back the tears. I'd always taken great pride in my belief that people were more important than possessions. "It's okay."

"No, it's not." He gathered me into his arms.

I relaxed for a minute against him, in an embrace as familiar to me as my own face in the mirror. At least this accident seemed to have chased away the stranger I'd been living with the last few days. My Phillip was back. Snuggled close to his heart, the smell of his soap filled my senses. I'd been right. People *were* more important than things.

I kept my head against his chest. "Will you have time to get the tree down before we do whatever you have planned for this afternoon?" Was it my imagination, or had his heartbeat quickened under my ear?

He pulled me to my feet. "We need to talk." My stomach flip-flopped as I followed him toward the sofa. This bore an eerie resemblance to the scene my friend Kathy had described when her husband had told her he was leaving her for another woman.

"The kids, too?" I nodded toward the thumping around upstairs, where Seth and Amanda were, no doubt, still gathering catalogs. If he wanted a divorce, he wouldn't want the kids there when he told me.

"I want to talk to you alone first."

Fighting the urge to run screaming from the room, I sat beside him on the sofa. A strange mix of determination and fear lurked in his blue eyes.

"Before you say anything," I stammered, my own heart hammering now, "I know things have been odd around here the last couple of months. You lost your job, and your dad had that heart attack. Thankfully, both ended up okay, but still, it was stressful for all of us. Now, the kids are just getting over their school problems and settling into homeschooling, and we're focused on the holidays. Plus, we're not used to having you home during the day."

I held up my hand and shook my head. That hadn't come out right. "Not that we don't like it. We do."

Fresh tears filled my eyes at the sympathetic look on his face. Phillip knew I babbled when I was nervous, and he'd always been very tenderhearted. If he was feeling sorry for me, it wasn't a good sign. "Phillip Seth Lassiter, don't you dare tell me you've fallen in love with a Peace Corps volunteer and are running away with her to live in a third-world country!"

Phillip burst out laughing. When he leaned across and hugged me, I clung to him like he was the last item on the shelf at Wal-Mart's day-after-Thanksgiving sale.

"My sweet, precious, hilarious Penny. You make it worth getting out of bed every day. Any man would be crazy to leave that."

Relief shot through me, fast and sharp. I grabbed his hand, squeezing it tight. "You scared me to death! Don't ever do that again."

"Well, my surprise does involve travel."

All this suspense over a vacation? I sighed. From Thanksgiving to Christmas was a busy whirl of parties and activities, but we could squeeze in a short family vacation. A long weekend, for sure. Maybe even a whole week.

"So, tell me! Where are we going?"

"Hmm. . .lots of places." To my amazement, he reached under a home decorating book on the coffee table and pulled out a travel atlas. He flipped the cover open to the big U.S. map and laid it on my lap.

Visions of romantic cruises and weekend getaways fled from my mind. A trail, marked in red, jumped off the page, winding hundreds of miles through the middle of the United States. "How will we do that? Even in a week, there's no way."

"No, but in a little over a month we can."

"A little over a month?" Had he lost his mind?

"Oh, Pen. It's going to be great."

I hadn't seen his eyes sparkle like that in so long, for a minute I had the breathless feeling I used to get when we were dating.

"I borrowed Bob and Sylvia's RV. Since they ended their retirement and bought the shop, they never use it. We'll haul the Mazda behind it for around-town trips." He held up a key with a grin. "We'll leave Monday."

So this is what it's like when your husband has a midlife crisis. That sparkle in his eyes clearly indicated insanity. My breathless feeling edged toward hyperventilation.

"We'll plan to be home right after New Year's Day. That will give us time to get settled in before I start my new job."

"Are you crazy?" My heart pounded, this time with anger instead of fear. "You expect me to miss Christmas with my folks?" A current of fury, strong enough to furnish power to our whole block, surged through my veins. I slapped the atlas, still open on my lap, and the sound reverberated through the room like a gunshot.

"Isn't that convenient? You wait until after I make Thanksgiving dinner for your parents before you spring this on me. We don't have to worry about letting *your* family down now." Heat flooded my face.

Richard and Janet Lassiter were like a second set of parents to me, and I knew Phillip felt the same way about my mom and dad. But I couldn't stop the hostile words. "Did you plan it that way?"

His face grew taut, but he didn't speak.

"Oh, Phillip." He knew how much I looked forward to Christmas. It wasn't just about spending the actual day with my folks. We'd also miss the weeks that led up to it—the delicious countdown to the big day. Why was he trying to spoil things for us? "What brought this on?"

"What brought this on is feeling like I barely know my kids." His eyes bore into mine. "And that they could care less whether I'm here or not, as long as I'm bringing home a paycheck so they can have the latest video game or the hottest fashion item."

The man who'd always laughingly compared me to

a mama tiger with her cubs really should have known better than to insult my kids.

I slammed the atlas shut and threw it on the table, watching through tear-dimmed eyes as it slid off the other side and hit the carpet with a dull thud. "That's not true and you know it!" My voice trembled. Amanda and Seth loved their father, and they were good kids. All of our friends talked about how blessed Phillip and I were to have such well-behaved children.

"It's not just the kids, Pen." He held his hands out in a gesture I recognized as an attempt to soothe me, but his words had the opposite effect. "You don't have time to even look up when I walk in the room. Unless it's to ask me to get something from the attic or run to the store."

"So, you're pouting and ruining Christmas because you feel ignored?" Red-hot anger boiled in my stomach at his childishness.

"No." He shook his head. "You know you're better with words than I am. Maybe I'm not explaining it very well." He reached for my hand, but I brushed away a tear to avoid his touch. "I want us to rediscover Christmas, not ruin it. I want us to rediscover each other. . .and God."

"God?" I laughed, almost a sob. "Phillip, we go to church three times a week. We never miss. When someone dies, I take food. You mow the church lawn when it's your turn. We both teach Bible class. People depend on us. What will God think about that if we go off on your big adventure?" I slapped my palms on my thighs and jumped to my feet. "I don't get this."

"This is important to me, Penny." He shoved to his feet, as well, and looked down at me. His eyes, so sparkly before, just looked sad. Hurt. "How many times have I ever asked you to do something big for me?"

Shaking, I turned and strode to the window where the Christmas tree should be going up right this minute. With my back to my husband, I stared out at our perfectly manicured yard. Phillip took care of it even when he was working fifty hours a week.

Shame mingled with my blinding anger. He was right. In sixteen years, easygoing Phillip had never asked for anything except my love, which I'd always assured him he had. Had the time come for me to put my money where my mouth was?

Chapter 2

...Two Pouting Kids

W hat do you say, Pen?"

I kept my back to him, tears stinging my eyes. "What *can* I say? It sounds like you've already decided."

"So you'll go?"

"Do I have a choice?" When we first married and I was learning what it meant for a wife to submit to her husband, every time we disagreed, I'd sarcastically pop off with, "Whatever you say. You're the boss." Phillip, trying to get the hang of loving his exasperating wife like he loved himself, would deflate before my eyes. I promised myself about five years into our marriage (okay, I'm a slow learner) that I'd never use that phrase again. And I hadn't. But, oh, how I wanted to now.

"We all have choices, Penny."

Really? Because, frankly, right now I don't see a plethora of options for me. "I'll go." I turned to face him.

Phillip's emotions were transparent. To me, at least. He wanted to push me for more, but he was afraid to.

Wise man. But was it too little wisdom, too late?

"Good. When should we tell the kids?"

"No time like the present," I said through gritted teeth.

Apparently deciding again to take my words at face value, he yelled up the stairs, "Seth, Amanda, come down here for a minute. Your mother and I have something to tell you."

"*You* have something to tell them," I whispered fiercely. "I don't."

He just glared at me. We stood in silence by the window, and a minute later, Seth bounded into the room with the limitless energy of a preadolescent boy. His hair stood on end, and he waved an Electronic City sale flyer. "I've found the remote control car I want. It's a real drag racer, and there's a new track out—" Something about our expressions, or the way his dad and I stood, together yet apart, made him stop just inside the doorway. "What's up?"

Before we could reply, Amanda walked in, her

arms filled with newspaper advertisements. She looked around the room. "Where's the tree?"

I stared out the window while Phillip told them his plan.

"I'm not going." Amanda threw the papers on the table and crossed her arms. "I'll stay with Emily."

I swung around to face her. Fat chance. Emily's parents thought fourteen was plenty old enough to be left alone at night. And if the girls wanted to go out, Emily's sixteen-year-old brother could drive them.

Before I could respond, Phillip squashed her plan. "This is not negotiable, Amanda. You *are* going."

She stared at him. I could almost see her looking at her little finger and thinking, *When did my dad come unwrapped?* Then she did what any normal teenage girl does when things go wrong. She shot *me* a venomous look, spun on her heel, and ran up the stairs.

"She's gotten way too big for her britches," Phillip muttered after her dramatic exit.

Seth had been quiet after Phillip's announcement, but he'd apparently learned something by her show of defiance.

"Dad," he said softly, "I'm not sure I'm really up to camping. I haven't been over the flu that long. Maybe I should stay at Grandma's."

Oh! I'm not feeling so great either. Think Grandma could

fit us both in? One look at Phillip's red face left little hope that Seth's approach was going to work any better than his sister's. Phillip didn't intend to make this trek alone.

"We're all going," Phillip said. He looked at me like he'd read my mind. "Every one of us."

Seth nodded and trudged up the stairs. Midway, he turned back. "What about our presents?"

What about your presents? What about your grandma and grandpa? And aunts and uncles and cousins? I screamed silently.

"We'll worry about presents when it gets closer to Christmas. There are stores on the road," Phillip answered.

Seth stomped up the stairs to his room and slammed his door.

After the kids were in bed, Phillip came into the kitchen where I was unloading the dishwasher. "Ready for bed?"

I placed a Corelle bowl in the top rack. "Well, you know I'll be heading out a little after five in the morning for the day-after sales. I thought I'd just sleep in the guest room so I won't wake you."

For a brief second, I wanted him to take me in his arms and tell me that he couldn't sleep without me next to him. We *never* slept apart unless someone was in the hospital.

He nodded.

Ever since he'd told me his crazy plan, he'd been like the little bobble-headed dog Amanda kept on her dresser. No matter what I said, he nodded. What had happened to the man who could charm the lemons off a lemon tree with his caring attitude?

Apparently that man was in hibernation.

Either that or he just didn't care anymore. Maybe he wanted to sleep alone. I slammed a fork into the silverware holder. Then there'd be no one to gripe when he kept his bedside lamp on studying the travel atlas.

"Do you have an alarm in there?"

"Huh?" I looked up and realized he was still standing by the counter. For a second I thought he meant in the dishwasher. "Oh. In the guest room? Yeah."

"Is Vicky going with you in the morning?"

It was my turn to nod, so I did. Maybe he *was* trying to get up the nerve to ask me not to sleep in the other room. Because that question was a no-brainer. My baby sister (all right, so thirty doesn't exactly qualify as a baby, but in our family it counts) has gone with me to the after-Thanksgiving sales since the year Phillip and I married and Vicky was still in braces.

It was our own special pre-Christmas ritual. One

that my mom and my older sister, Sandy, couldn't understand since they thought no early morning bargain was worth leaving a warm bed for, but Vicky and I loved the challenge. Thankfully, we lived in the same suburb of Little Rock, so neither of us had to drive far to keep our tradition.

Since Phillip still stood there silently, I decided to expound. "I'm going to pick her up."

He nodded. In sixteen years, we'd not nodded as much as we had tonight. Was this what couples did when they didn't talk? No wonder my chiropractor's waiting room was always full. Silent arguments had to be a strain on people's necks.

"Okay, y'all be careful. Good night." He swooped in for a kiss just as I put a plate in the bottom rack. He ended up connecting with my hair.

"Good night." When his footsteps faded away, I leaned against the counter. I could count on one hand the number of times we'd ever gone to bed angry. And even in those times, we always woke in the morning in the familiar spoon position. It was hard to stay mad when you were snuggled up against someone.

I reached for my vitamins and admitted something to myself. I *wanted* to stay mad at Phillip. I felt righteous in my anger, and it seemed almost as if getting over it would be wrong. I knew that was silly. *Behold—the convoluted reasoning of Penny Lassiter.*

My righteous anger made a poor bed partner. According to the law of thermostat control, every room in our house should have been the same temperature. But the guest room was like the inside of an ice cube.

When I finally drifted off to sleep, I instinctively scooted over to cuddle up to Phillip. Every time I'd move from my warm spot into the wasteland of cold sheet beside me, I'd wake and the process would start over again.

This exercise in futility went on all night. When the alarm buzzed at four thirty, I was ready for a warm shower.

Driving toward Vicky's house, I decided to pass the whole trip thing off as a lark. Even though I was furious at Phillip, it went against my grain to talk bad about him to someone else.

I'd spent a good ten years training him to be loyal to me. (Oh, I don't mean as in faithful. He had that down pat from the beginning. I mean, as in not talking about me to other people in an unflattering way, even if it was intended as a joke.) The last thing I wanted to be was a hypocrite.

Vicky climbed into the car with the grace of a gazelle, and as usual, I fought a bit of envy. It was a good thing I loved her so much, because I might be tempted to hate her otherwise. She was a natural beauty, and everything seemed to come easy to her. On days like today, that bothered me a little, but most of the time I was glad for her.

"Hi."

"Good morning."

If I were a betting woman, I'd say she'd rolled right out of bed and into her clothes, remembering at the last minute to pull her blond mane up on top of her head in one of those bear-claw clips. She looked incredible.

"Been up long?"

She flashed me a rueful grin. "About three minutes."

"Want to stop at McDonald's?"

"I'm not sure they're open yet. Let's do Wal-Mart first and then drive through Mickey Dee's for breakfast on the way to the mall."

I nodded and smiled as I headed to Wal-Mart. Vicky and I had this conversation every year. At least some things stayed the same. If Phillip were here, we'd probably have to eat breakfast at Taco Bell, just to be different. My smile faded as I remembered the cold guest room bed. That had certainly been different.

"Penny, are you okay?"

I looked over at Vicky. "Sure, I'm fine. Why?"

She snorted. "I asked you if you thought Sandy and Bart would like the DVD player."

I pulled up to a stoplight. Had she lost her mind? Maybe she and Phillip had caught the same mysterious disease. "Vicky, we draw individual names in our family. We have a price limit. Why would you decide to buy Sandy and Bart a DVD player?"

"Penny." Her tone of voice was similar to one she might use with her three-year-old. "I just told you. I drew Sandy's name and Tony got Bart's. That was my question. Should we get them separate gifts like normal, or pool the money we'd spend and get them a DVD player together?"

"Oh. Yeah, that would be fine."

"What's wrong with you?" She crossed her arms, and even in the dim light of early dusk, I recognized the bulldog expression on her face.

"We've had a little change of plans at our house," I said in my most cheerful tone. "About Christmas, I mean." I pulled into one of the few empty parking places in the crowded lot and killed the motor. I could feel Vicky looking at me, so I fumbled in my purse, making a show of counting off the important items— my checkbook, my wallet, and oh, yes, for all those 6:00 a.m. calls I get, my cell phone.

"Pen. What are you talking about?"

Before I could answer, she continued.

"Miss Never-Change-a-Thing Penny has had a

change of plans for Christmas?" Her voice squeaked on the last word.

So much for making the trip sound like a lark. I could feel the tears welling, and I was afraid if I made her drag it out of me, the DVD players would be gone when we got in there. Not to mention the things on *my* list. So I spilled the whole story right there in the Wal-Mart parking lot.

"That's not so bad, Penny. It might be fun."

Fun? Didn't she hear the part about us leaving in three days? And missing Christmas at Mom's?

"Yeah, it'll be a blast." I snatched a Kleenex from my purse. "How would you like it if Tony planned a trip during the holidays without asking you?"

"If it meant he was spending time with me and the kids instead of working all the time, I'd be willing to go to the wilds of Africa for Christmas." Her wistful tone cooled my anger quickly. Tony loved her, but he was a workaholic. Even though he'd wanted children, they were completely Vicky's responsibility.

"Won't you miss us?" The squeezing feeling in my chest was back as I thought of them all gathering for Christmas without us.

"Oh, Penny." She hugged me tightly. "You know we will. It'll be awful. What in the world is Phillip thinking?"

That's more like it.

I cried in her arms for a few minutes while she patted my back. Then I thought of the name she'd called me. I jerked away and looked out the window.

"What?" she asked, exasperation creeping into her voice. *We got up at the crack of dawn to make this sale,* I could almost hear her thinking.

"Am I really what you said? Miss Never Change—whatever?" I blew my nose.

"Sure, you are, but that's okay." She grabbed her purse. "Come on, it'll all work out. Let's go buy some coffeepots and electric knives. You'll feel better and for five dollars each, how can we go wrong?"

I got out of the car like a good sport, and didn't tell her that, thanks to my unwillingness to break traditions, I still had three coffeepots, one can opener, and two electric knives from last year's after-Thanksgiving sale. Not to mention my stash in the attic from years past.

No sense ruining Vicky's fun.

Chapter 3

...*Three Days to Pack*

By Friday night, my resentment had settled. Not settled as in dissipated, but settled as in settled in for a long winter's nap.

I snatched another Christmas sweatshirt from the drawer and tossed it on top of the pile of clothes. The half-full suitcase, open on the bed, was already a sea of red and green. I'd pulled out every holiday shirt I owned to take on *Phillip's* trip. *Let him see if he can skip Christmas with Holly Holiday as a traveling companion.*

Submissive was one thing, but there was nothing that said I had to be nice about it. In my mind's eye, I could see Jiminy Cricket saying something about those Scriptures I'd used when I'd taught a ladies' Bible class on submission a few months ago. I grabbed an imaginary flyswatter, and he quickly disappeared. I was going, wasn't I? What more could anyone expect?

Amanda had barely come out of her room since the announcement. Every time I'd passed her door, I could hear her on the phone, whispering to her friends. But when I asked her if she was okay, she just nodded and shut her bedroom door. Not slammed it, of course, but closed it very pointedly, with injured dignity.

Seth wasn't much better. He'd asked a million questions about the RV. They boiled down to one thing. Would he be able to take his electronic stuff with him? I'd used a very sweet tone when I told him to ask his dad. After all, the RV was his department.

"Pen?"

I looked up from my packing to meet Phillip's concerned gaze. He stood in the doorway as if afraid to come into his own bedroom. "Yeah?"

"This trip would be a lot more fun if you weren't mad at me."

Mad? Me, mad? I could feel a vein in my forehead pulsing as I finished folding the shirt. *Could a thirty-five-year-old woman have an anger-induced stroke?* I fixed my gaze on the doorframe to the right of his head. "I agreed to go."

He opened his mouth, then shook his head. "I was

hoping for a little more enthusiasm than that."

I didn't speak but went back to my folding and packing as if he weren't still there. He stood for a minute, and I knew he was watching me. Finally, I felt him move on down the hallway.

Still holding a green sweatshirt with a big gold ornament emblazoned on the front, I glanced at the empty doorway. "And *I* was hoping for a normal Christmas," I muttered.

"What?" How could I have forgotten that this was the man who could hear coins jingle in my change purse when I bought a blouse at the mall five miles away?

"Just talking to myself." I held my breath, half afraid, half hopeful he'd come back and insist on having a confrontation.

I heard him tap on Amanda's door instead. *Divide and conquer? Is that his plan now?* My face grew hot at the unjust thought. I tucked the last Christmas shirt in the suitcase and sank down on the bed.

My stomach hadn't stopped burning since the startling announcement yesterday, in spite of the fact that I'd raided the medicine cabinet and taken Phillip's antacids captive. I reached into my cardigan pocket and shook the hostage bottle lightly. He'd need them after the pizza I'd ordered for supper.

I would gladly give them back if he'd call this whole

crazy trip off. Maybe I should write a note and tell him that. He used to love it when I made him laugh.

Or maybe I should just take two more antacids. If I didn't find some peace about this, I'd have an ulcer by New Year's.

My prayers didn't seem to be getting anywhere, and I couldn't help but wonder if it was because they all started with, *Dear God, please change Phillip's mind.*

I figured Phillip's were the same, except he inserted my name, of course. I could almost see our prayers colliding headlong in the attic and canceling each other out. Which didn't leave much hope for a happy household.

I didn't want to sleep in the guest room again, but I didn't want to face Phillip either, so, knowing he always watched the ten o'clock news in the den, I slipped up to our room a few minutes before nine and got ready for bed. By nine-thirty, I was lying in the dark.

Unfortunately, I'd never been more wide awake.

My mind whirled with the things that still had to be done before we left. I grabbed a notepad and pen from my nightstand and, by flashlight, wrote my to-do list.

Cancel the newspaper.
Pay bills.
Call Lynette and tell her I won't be hosting our
ladies' Bible study ornament exchange this year.

Call Tracey and have her get someone else to make
the gingerbread hunting lodge for Seth's Boy
Scout party. Offer recipe from last year.
Call Susan and ask her to organize the
mother/daughter outlet mall trip. Remind her
to be sure everyone has a chance to buy a
coupon booklet at the mall office.
Call Mom—

Tears stung my eyes. *What will I tell her?* She loved Phillip like a son. How could I say, "Mom, apparently my husband has turned into a pod person and now he doesn't want to be with y'all this year. He'd rather—"? Before I could finish the imaginary, though heartbreaking, conversation, I heard footsteps approaching. I switched off the flashlight and slid the list under my pillow.

"Pen?"

I forced my breathing to even out.

He stood at the foot of the bed for a few seconds, then went on to the bathroom. Just as I finished saying my silent prayers, I heard the bathroom door open and felt his weight on the bed. He turned toward the wall and stayed on his own side. Irrational anger shot through me. The tears that had threatened earlier fell onto my pillow. Within minutes, he was snoring.

I had an overpowering urge to hit him. *Hard.*

Chapter 4

. . .Four Rolling Wheels

Monday came in much the same manner as my thirtieth birthday had five years earlier, like a mischievous little kid forcing me to play when I didn't want to. *"Ready or not, here I come."*

After two nights of going to sleep on the edge of the bed and two mornings of waking up in the curve of Phillip's warm embrace, my anger had waned a little. . .until the gathering rain clouds and my teenage daughter decided to compete to see which could cry the hardest.

Amanda's two closest friends showed up to see her off before they caught the bus to school and she caught the RV to the land of broken dreams. The three of them huddled on the porch, sobbing together. The sky cried with them, and I wanted to but refrained.

I stepped into the house and shook the water from my umbrella just as Phillip came up from the basement. I cast a pointed glance out the window toward Amanda, then gave him a look that spoke volumes.

"Did you see that girl's eyebrow ring?" he asked. "You should be glad to get Amanda away from that for a while."

"Emily will still be here when we get back, Phillip."

"From the way they're carrying on, you'd think we were going to be gone a year," he muttered as he locked the basement door.

"When you're fourteen, there's very little difference between a month and a year." I checked the coffeepot again to be sure it was unplugged. We'd loaded the RV the night before, so all we had to do was go. In theory. In reality, I had to check and double-check everything.

"When I was fourteen, I would have been thrilled if my parents had planned a trip like this. I don't see why Seth and Amanda have to be so obstinate."

"Just for the record, their 'parents' didn't plan this trip. Their 'father' did." I kept meaning to keep my mouth shut so we wouldn't fight, but every time he said something, the words just tumbled out.

"That's right. And they should be thankful."

I snorted. Phillip strode from the room without looking back.

I stepped into the den. I still couldn't believe that, for the first time in the history of our house, it was going to be undecorated until next year. Assuming His Highness allowed us to stay home then. Who knew? We might be going to the moon for the holidays next year.

Tears filled my eyes for the umpteenth time. I despised my bitter anger almost as much as I hated missing Christmas. I'd always been so easygoing. Hadn't I? Or had the going just been easy?

No. We'd had hard times. Like the miscarriage before Amanda was born. And not nearly as bad but still awful, the college days when only a bag of potatoes and a few cans of Campbell's soup stood between us and starvation. But we'd clung together, co-victims of circumstance.

Since Phillip was the perpetrator in the crime of turning our lives upside down, it was difficult to cling to him.

I picked up the fluffy towel from the floor and tossed it over the couch arm. At least, he'd put the Christmas ornaments back in the attic, so I didn't have to face doing that. I tried to be grateful for that crumb of sensitivity on his part, but the spot in front of the window stood out like a missing diamond ring after a broken engagement.

"You ready?" Phillip called from the hall.

Even though he couldn't see me, I nodded and turned off the den light. *Might as well be.* "Are the kids loaded?"

"Amanda's still saying good-bye, but Seth is settling in."

Seth was adapting better than Amanda, partly because his daddy had allowed him to take his hand-held electronic game. Technology appealed to Seth more than people did, which is the main reason we'd decided to start homeschooling him.

I'd grown tired of treating black eyes and busted lips from kids who called him a "geek" or worse. *"Grown tired" sounds so long-suffering, and that might be misleading. The truth is, no one will ever know how close I came to ending up the lead story on the six o'clock news: "Vigilante Mama Makes Playground Bullies Eat Dirt."*

"Are you about ready?" Phillip asked from the doorway.

"I guess so."

He must have been encouraged by the sleep-induced snuggling because he put his arms around me and leaned down to kiss me. I slammed my nose against his top button and felt his lips brush the top of my hair.

"Penny, I can't stand this."

It's not too late to call it all off. Before I said it aloud, my heart sank. *Am I really submitting if I manipulate him into doing what I want him to?*

"Can't stand what? We're doing what you wanted," I said to his button.

He didn't speak, but he also didn't push me away in disgust. I rested my ear against his chest, listening to his heartbeat for the second time in a week. I guess I needed reassurance that he hadn't really turned into an alien. I hardly ever got quiet enough or still enough to hear anyone's heart, but this morning I was in no hurry to go anywhere.

The constant *thump, thump, thump* drained away some of the irritation (I know; I'm the queen of understatement) I'd been carrying around the past few days. My husband was as solid and steady as his heartbeat. Why was I worried about giving him a month of my life?

Fine, my inner child whined, *but does it have to be the month that includes Christmas?* As much as her whining got on my nerves, this time I couldn't keep from agreeing with her.

"Penny."

I stepped back to look up at him, but either Phillip was afraid I'd bolt, or he liked me in spite of my. . . ahem. . .irritation, because he kept his hands on my waist. "Yeah?"

"This isn't going to be as bad as you think. Are you

sure you don't want to know where we're going and what I have planned for us?"

"I'm sure." I'd made that plain to him as soon as he'd started waving the travel atlas around and talking about KOA campgrounds. But even though he was acting like a total rat, after sixteen years of enjoying his crooked grin, I couldn't take another second of the worry shadowing his face. I gave him a quick hug and forced a smile. "Surprise me."

He took advantage of my upturned face and swooped in for the first kiss since Thursday afternoon that hadn't landed on my hair.

"I intend to surprise you. . .over and over again," he murmured against my lips.

"Humph. In an RV with the whole family? Fat chance." I pulled away from him and smoothed down my red and green sweatshirt.

He grinned and opened the door, ushering me out. *Is he being gallant, or is he just afraid I'll change my mind and run back to the bedroom and lock myself in?*

The wind had picked up and the rain was blowing on the porch, so Amanda and her friends pressed against the wall. When we came out the door, she sniffed and turned her back on us.

In some bizarre twist of fate, I was bearing the brunt of her displeasure more than Phillip. Tears mingled with

154

the rain hitting my face. Ever since we'd pulled her out of school to homeschool, she'd looked forward to this holiday with her friends so much. Not that she'd told me, but I'd gathered it from bits of conversations I'd heard—usually right before she rolled her eyes at me and closed her door or lowered her voice to a whisper.

Phillip tapped Amanda on the shoulder. "Come on, honey, it's time to go." The firmness in his voice was unmistakable, and Amanda knew better than to argue. She hugged her friends one more time, and they splashed down the driveway to wait for the school bus, huddling together under a piece of black plastic.

I leaned toward Amanda with my umbrella, but she shrugged it off and stomped through the rain to the RV. I knew I should be mad, and I *was* aggravated that she wouldn't give an inch, but a large part of me wanted to hand Phillip the umbrella and stomp right along behind her.

"Don't worry. She'll come around."

I just shook my head and followed Amanda.

Phillip pulled the motor home door shut behind us.

Seth sat in the chair behind the driver's seat playing his GameBoy. Amanda dripped on the welcome mat. Every morning she painstakingly straightened her long blond hair with a blow-dryer. Thanks to her belligerent tromp through the rain, she looked like a combination of Medusa and a teenage Shirley Temple.

Phillip passed her a large towel. She jutted her chin, and for a second I thought she would refuse, but maybe she'd learned from the umbrella incident because she snatched the towel from his hand as forcefully as she dared.

He sank into the captain's chair that served as a driver seat by day and a comfy recliner by night and swiveled to face us. "I thought we'd pray before we start."

Amanda stopped in midtoweling, and for the first time since I'd entered the RV, Seth tore his gaze from his handheld game. Normally, at our house, prayers were reserved for meals and bedtime.

As my own emotions roiled, I looked out the window at the relentless rain and then at Amanda's stormy expression. "I think prayer is a great idea."

Chapter 5

...Five Hundred Miles

After the prayer, Amanda plopped down in her chair, buckled in, and used the towel to cover her face. Reality hit me like a punch—we were really doing this. I hadn't been able to talk Phillip out of this mad trip. I sank onto the love seat and fastened my seat belt.

A few minutes later, Phillip breezed merrily onto the I-440 loop, whistling the chorus to "On the Road Again." How I wished I were a fly on the wall of that man's brain. Where had he gotten this sudden determination to do his own thing?

He'd never been exactly passive, but I think I'd imagined that whatever my desires in life were, his were the same. I glanced at the thick portfolio beside him on the console. Maps, sticky notes, and printouts of e-mails bulged out the edges. That notebook may have been the most amazing revelation of all. For the past sixteen years, Phillip couldn't even order pizza without me. How had he gathered all of that information?

Last week, right before I'd thrown the atlas across the room, I'd noticed a red circle of sorts. I did a mental geography review. We were headed east, so my best guess is that we were on our way to Memphis.

Amanda is a huge Elvis fan. (Okay, I admit it. I'm a little fascinated with the hip-swiveling king myself.) We'd always planned to go to Graceland, and no doubt, Phillip thought he'd start the trip off right by taking us there. I smirked. I'd figured out his first surprise without even breaking a sweat.

Maybe I could pretend for the next few days we were just on a short vacation in Memphis. Who knows? If we got along well and showered him with attention, maybe Phillip would go along with my new plan—thinning out his notebook and heading home ahead of schedule. Like three and a half weeks ahead of schedule.

We'd buzz in, do Graceland, hit the malls, and get home in time to enjoy the Christmas things I'd had to give up. Sounded like a plan.

"Humph," I snorted. Who was I kidding? The nice comfortable man I'd married had turned into a man of steel. I'd have a better chance convincing Superman to let the two trains crash and just spend time with me than I would convincing this new Phillip to change his plans.

"What are you grunting about?" Phillip's blue eyes twinkled in the rearview mirror.

"Nothing, really. Just thinking."

"About what?"

I glanced at the kids. Amanda appeared to be sound asleep, although her wild curls covered her face, so I couldn't be sure. Seth had put on his headphones after I'd objected to the annoying sound on his electronic game.

I waited for a traffic lull, then hurried into the passenger seat and buckled in. "Thinking about you." I could at least try to talk him into the Memphis-then-home idea.

He raised his eyebrows. "What about me?"

"Just wondering why you're doing this. Really."

The twinkle fled from his eyes like a blown-out birthday candle. "You know why. But you won't let yourself really see."

Talking to him was an obvious dead end, so I dug in my bag and got out the Heartsong romances that had come in the mail Friday. I hadn't even had time to look at any of the four since then, but I quickly picked one and lost myself in the pages until we stopped at a roadside park.

I fixed sandwiches, but it was raining too hard to get out of the RV. Seth played his game while he ate, and I didn't have the heart to stop him. Amanda maintained her stoic silence. So I read my book. Phillip tried a couple of conversation starters, but when they fell flat, he picked up his beloved travel atlas.

After lunch, I took my post next to Phillip again, but since I wasn't really speaking to him, I couldn't seem to fight the sleepiness—too many nights of trying to stay on my own side of the bed, I guess.

"Penny?" Phillip's voice sounded a long way off.

"Hmm?"

"We're about two hours from where we're going to stop for the night. But there's a gas station coming up. Do you need to stop?"

"I don't care." I opened one eye. We weren't on the interstate anymore. Nothing looked familiar. "Are we almost to Memphis?" *Oops.* So much for keeping my discovery about our destination a secret. I hate it when I talk before I'm totally awake. *Never a good idea.*

He glanced at me and frowned. "We bypassed Memphis about thirty minutes ago."

Bypassed Memphis? Why would any sane person do that? Oh, I forgot.

I shushed my inner child but not before I heard her wail, *What about the mall? And Graceland? Just when I was dreaming of Elvis in crushed velvet!* "Where are we now?" I asked.

"Almost to Holly Springs."

"Holly Springs what?"

He kept his gaze on the road, but I could see his right eyebrow rise. "Mississippi. Are you sure you don't want to know the itinerary? This is the last time I'm going to offer."

Have you ever heard that expression cutting off your nose to spite your face? Well, in addition to being the queen of understatement, I'm also the duchess of cutting off my nose.

"I told you to surprise me."

"Fine. You can count on it." With his right hand, he slid the bulging black notebook from the console and put it between his seat and the wall.

Phillip knew me too well. When I calmed down, I'd regret not letting him tell me. A surreptitious peek at the contents of that portfolio would be much easier on my ego than asking him to fill me in on the details later.

I drifted back to sleep and didn't rouse until two

hours later when we pulled into an RV park.

"We're here," Phillip boomed cheerfully.

I bit back a sarcastic remark. In that drowsy place between dream and wake that I like to call the land of good intentions, I'd promised myself I was going to start thinking positive about this trip. That included not making sarcastic remarks to the driver.

"It's not raining nearly as hard." Okay, so my comment wasn't exactly exuberant, but it *was* positive.

"Where are we?" Amanda pushed her hair back from her face. She'd slept most of the day. When she had been awake, she'd stared out the window silently like a modern-day Joan of Arc on her way to the stake.

"We're at a campground," Seth answered. He pressed his face against the glass and stared at the little kiosk we'd pulled up next to. A man in a guard uniform stood at the window.

"In Tupelo, Mississippi," Phillip added and then gave the guard at the window his name. "This is where we're going to camp the next few days."

"Why?" Amanda dropped the blinds on her window in disgust. "It doesn't look very exciting."

"Looks can be deceiving." Phillip took the map and papers and drove a few hundred yards. He hopped out, freed the Mazda, and then smoothly backed the RV into its temporary resting place. He beamed like he'd manually hooked us back up with the saucer section of the Enterprise.

"Seth, you and your sister need to help me get things set up outside."

"Great," Amanda said. "Slopping around in the rain is my idea of fun."

"You didn't seem to mind it this morning when you wouldn't take your mom's umbrella."

I cast Phillip a "Hey-leave-me-out-of-it" look.

"Won't we get wet?" Seth asked.

"There are some slickers in the drawer. Get them on and let's get going."

I kicked around the idea of offering to help, but I decided fixing supper by myself was enough of a sacrifice, even if it was just tuna salad sandwiches.

They came in thirty minutes later, hung their dripping ponchos to dry, and dove into the sandwiches like they were a five-course meal. After we finished eating, Phillip rubbed his hands together and smiled. "Who wants to go for a drive around Tupelo?"

I picked at the sleeve of my Christmas tree cardigan. "I think I'll stay here and get our beds ready."

Amanda curled her lip. "Sounds like more excitement than I can stand. I guess I'll just stay here."

"I'll pass." Seth was already engrossed in his game again.

If Phillip was disappointed by our desertion, he hid it well. "Okay. I've got to check on some things for tomorrow, but I'll be back in an hour or so."

Seth looked up. "Tomorrow? What are we doing tomorrow?"

"Oh." Phillip grabbed the car keys from a hook by the door. His grin never faltered, but his blue eyes bore into mine. "It's a surprise."

The next morning, the cell-phone alarm buzzed at six. I think it's safe to say we were all surprised.

Phillip leaped from the bed and pulled on some jogging pants and a T-shirt. "Let's go get a shower."

I blinked. " 'Let's'?"

He grinned. "No, that's not the surprise. Although, now that you mention it. . ." He raised his eyebrow and winked.

I glared at him.

He laughed. "They have a shower house. And thanks to my careful planning, we're parked right next to it. We can all shower at the same time."

"Joy."

Obviously impervious to my sarcasm, he lumbered down the hall to wake the kids. "What should I wear?" I called.

"Whatever you brought will be fine. Forget it, Penny. I'm not giving any hints. You wanted it that way, remember?" He turned his attention back to Seth.

I scrambled to my feet. Now where had he hidden that black notebook?

Chapter 6

. . .Six Hours Working

I didn't find Phillip's itinerary, so I was more than a little shocked Tuesday morning when we parked the Mazda in front of a large, red brick church building on Elm Street. Phillip turned to Seth and Amanda. "You two get to be babysitters today."

They groaned.

Phillip held up his hand in a crossing-guard gesture. He very rarely did that, but when he did, the kids both knew there would be no arguments. "They really need you. There are several children coming." He smiled. "Besides, it'll be fun, and you won't be on your own. There'll be an adult around to help you."

He got out of the car and strode to the building.

I couldn't even look at Seth and Amanda. I knew they were completely stunned, and I was afraid they'd recognize the same emotion in me. We were going to leave our children with a stranger to look after other strangers' children?

I grabbed Phillip's shirt just as he touched the door handle. "Can I talk to you for a minute?" I said softly.

He turned to me. "Yes, but before you ask, Tommy's the preacher here. His wife will be with the kids."

Tommy's wife? We'd never met Ronda in person, but Phillip and Tommy had been friends since college, and we'd exchanged Christmas cards for years.

It occurred to me that maybe Phillip's scheming had something to do with wanting to be alone with me for the day. I relaxed.

I was glad Phillip hadn't allowed Seth to bring the GameBoy this morning. He'd have no choice but to talk to the other kids. And maybe a day of babysitting would show Amanda that the world didn't revolve around her.

Phillip stared at me, one eyebrow raised.

What did this man have up his sleeve? "Okay."

His smile drove every cloud from the sky. "Great."

We met Ronda, then left while she showed the kids around the fellowship hall where they would be watching the children.

"Is there a mother's shopping trip planned today?"

I asked Phillip on the way out to the car.

"Something like that."

We stopped at McDonald's half a mile from the church and ate a relaxed breakfast. Through unspoken agreement, we didn't mention the road trip, but Phillip amused me with stories of his and Tommy's college antics.

We left the restaurant and had only driven a few blocks when Phillip pulled into a driveway that already held several vehicles. The medium-sized house had partially finished vinyl siding, and I could see two men up on the roof with hammers.

"Umm. . .Phillip?" The bottom dropped out of my stomach. Had he built us a new house in Tupelo, Mississippi, without telling me? These days anything was possible. "What are we doing here?"

"The church is doing a house-raising. And we're just in time to help."

So much for him wanting to spend a day alone with me. "A house what?"

"Like an old-fashioned barn raising. Only this is a house."

"Why?"

"Well, a member had a house fire and no insurance."

I wanted to ask why again, but I didn't. Instead I only asked the more pressing question. "Why do they need us?"

"They have no place to live. The church members are building them a new house. Ronda and our children are babysitting the workers' kids today. I told Tommy we'd help, too." He unfastened his seat belt and touched my hand. "Unless you don't want to?"

Talk about being backed into a corner. If I said I didn't want to, what kind of person—what kind of Christian—would I be? But the truth was, the only thing I really wanted to do right now was throw myself on my bed for a good long cry. Unfortunately, my bed was several hundred miles in the opposite direction. *At least I still have a bed.* "That'll be fine."

Phillip smiled like I'd won the Nobel Peace Prize. "Good. Wonderful."

We were each assigned a partner and a task as soon as we walked in the door. The only bright spot in the day was my tile-laying partner, Donita. She was hilarious. Her self-deprecating humor put me so much at ease that after a short lunch break, I found myself telling her about our trip. . .starting with Phillip's Thanksgiving Day announcement.

She sympathized as we painstakingly cut the peel-and-stick vinyl tiles to fit. After I finished my story, I sat back on my heels. "It could have been worse. At first I thought he was leaving me for another woman."

She nodded. "Been there, done that, got the divorce

papers. It was the real deal for me."

"Oh, Donita, I'm so sorry."

She shook her head. "Don't be sorry for me, girl. Be sorry for him. I've always said there wasn't another human being on earth that would be worth me giving up going to sleep in the same house as my children every night. He used to think that, too. But somewhere along the path to 'as long as we both shall live,' he lost his way." She smiled and crow's-feet crinkled at the corners of her eyes. "You pray for him if you get a chance, okay?"

I nodded. *How could any man have left her for someone else? Her beauty is way more than skin-deep.*

Within a minute, she was cracking another joke, and I was laughing.

Six hours after Phillip and I arrived, Donita and I finished. I hugged her tightly and assured her I'd pray for her whole family, including her ex-husband.

"God will bless you for what you did today, Penny. Trust Phillip. He's a good man. He knows what he's doing."

When we were on our way to pick up the kids, Phillip looked over at me. "What do you think?"

"After laying tile all day, I'm so sore I can hardly move. What about you?"

"I'm tired, too, but it felt good to help."

"Yeah." I thought of the volunteers working so unselfishly. "I just hope the owners appreciate the huge amount of sweat equity that is going into their new home."

He frowned. "Didn't Donita seem appreciative to you?"

"Donita?"

He nodded. "The house is for her and her three kids."

My new friend, Donita, had recently lost her house in a fire? Less than a year after her husband walked out on her?

"I can't believe she didn't tell you."

"Me either." *And all I did was complain.*

As Phillip and I drove to the church building to get the kids, I silently replayed my conversations with Donita. Could someone really be that strong in the face of such adversity?

Um. . .Lord? I'm tired of my selfish heart. Could I get one like Donita's instead?

As soon as I thought the prayer, I started mentally backpedaling. I didn't want to lose my husband in order to get a new heart. Or my house. I sighed. But if those things ever happened, I wanted to face them with the kind of faith Donita seemed to possess.

When Seth and Amanda climbed into the car, they

looked as tired as I felt. Phillip grinned. "How did babysitting go?" he asked.

They looked at each other. "It was okay," Seth said. He nodded toward Amanda. "Except *she* wouldn't stop being bossy."

Amanda gasped. "I was not bossy. You were going to let Annie climb up higher than she should have. All I did was tell you not to."

He crossed his arms. "That's what I call bossy."

"Whatever." Amanda shrugged.

"I accept your apology," Seth said.

I looked sideways at Phillip, and he nodded slightly in agreement. Good comeback.

Amanda chose to ignore it. (Or maybe "whatever" *was* the new "I'm sorry." What did I know?) "It was actually harder than I thought it would be. Especially when Jeffie got that extra-large crayon stuck up his nose."

"Mrs. Wilson says he does that all the time. Travis crumbled cookies in Alexis's hair." Seth made a crumbling motion with his hands.

"Oh, gross. How did you get it out?" Amanda asked.

For the rest of the trip to the RV park, they talked about the kids they'd watched. I smiled as they compared notes about who whined the most and who screamed the loudest when it was time to wash their hands. I couldn't remember the last time I'd heard them actually have a conversation. Maybe this had been a great way to start off our trip.

I cast a sideways glance at Phillip. *Kudos to the itinerary planner.* Wonder what else he had scheduled in that elusive notebook of his?

The next day, Phillip gave us a choice. Going back to help on Donita's house another day, which meant babysitting again for Seth and Amanda, or moving on. The kids weren't enthusiastic about either option, but to my amazement, before I could cast my ballot, they voted to stay and help. As sore as my muscles were, I was kind of glad I hadn't had to decide.

The second night, we attended a Bible study at the Elm Street church with the people we'd come to know so well the past couple of days. After we got back to the RV, I fell into bed exhausted. Right before I drifted off, I remembered that if we were at home I would have been hosting the Secret Santa swap for my book group. I would be the proud owner of a new book. (We were predictable. We always gave each other books.) But I wouldn't have been able to help Donita have four newly tiled floors.

The next morning, after a leisurely breakfast, Phillip

surprised us with a trip to Elvis's birthplace. It wasn't Graceland, but Amanda and I were thrilled, and even Seth was impressed.

We headed out of Tupelo around noon up the Natchez Trace Parkway. Our tour guide (Phillip) told us a little of the history of the centuries-old road.

"Mom," Amanda asked about half an hour after leaving Elvis's childhood home, "did you know Elvis had a twin who died at birth?"

"I guess I'd heard it a long time ago, but I'd forgotten it." For a change of pace, I'd allowed her to sit with me on the love seat as long as we both wore our seat belts.

"It must have been awful for his mom and dad," Seth offered with surprising insight.

"Yeah, but at least they still had Elvis."

"One baby doesn't take the place of another one, though, sweetie," Phillip spoke from the driver's seat without turning around. "We love you and Seth, but the baby we lost before we had you will always be precious to us."

Amanda stared at me, wide-eyed. "You lost a baby before me?"

I felt a twinge of irritation at Phillip. I'd always thought there was no point in sharing our sorrow with the kids, considering it had happened before they were born.

"Yes. A boy," Phillip answered, keeping his eyes on the road.

"I had a brother?" Seth asked.

"His name was Jared," Phillip volunteered, a regular fount of information.

"Was he stillborn like Elvis's twin?" Amanda asked.

"Actually, I miscarried—" At the look of confusion on Seth's face, I clarified. "He was born way too early, and he was too little to live in the world." Tears edged my eyes and the familiar lump filled my throat. "But we sure did love him."

Amanda leaned her head over on my shoulder. To my amazement, she had tears in her eyes, too. Had I been wrong to protect them from our loss?

We rode in silence for a while, but I noticed Seth didn't pick his game up again.

"Did you see that deer?" he called out.

Amanda and I turned around to look, and sure enough, a big buck stood by the side of the road, almost as if waiting for us to go by so he could cross the parkway.

"Look! He has a family just like us." Amanda pointed to the woods behind the buck, where a doe and two smaller deer eyed our motor home.

"Nobody has a family just like us," I quipped.

Amanda glanced at Seth and her dad and rolled her eyes at me. "That's for sure."

Chapter 7

...Seven Wieners Roasting

Traveling the Natchez Trace Parkway was like stepping back in time. No billboards, no neon signs, and slower-than-normal speed limits. We took occasional breaks along the way to walk on the original trail or soak in the view from an overlook. In spite of their grumbling, Seth and Amanda were the first ones out of the RV every time.

Late that afternoon, we stopped at the Meriwether Lewis Burial Site. "Why don't we camp here?" Phillip said while we were reading about the monument.

"Eww! You've got to be kidding!" Amanda shivered. "We're going to spend the night at a burial site?"

Phillip laughed, but frankly, I thought it was a valid question.

"No, at the campground over there."

I gave a small sigh of relief. I'd learned the hard way on this trip never to assume.

After we had the RV set up, Phillip looked around. "Who wants to help me build a fire?"

"Outside?" Seth asked, amazed.

"No. On your bunk," Amanda drawled.

Seth's face turned red.

Amanda stared at her brother. "I was just teasing." She rolled her eyes and punched his arm. "Come on. Might as well."

"How about you, Pen?" Phillip asked.

"I think I'll start supper."

"Hey," Seth yelled from the doorway, "can we roast hot dogs? Like on TV?"

"And marshmallows?" Amanda added as she followed her brother outside.

Roasting hot dogs and marshmallows had been such a large part of my growing up. When had it become easier to just order pizza? I couldn't believe my kids had never experienced a wiener roast.

"There *is* a bag of marshmallows in the cabinet," Phillip said.

I smiled at the thought. "And I have a whole pack

of hot dogs in the fridge."

Phillip offered a sheepish grin. "Not quite a whole pack. I ate a cold one for a midnight snack the other night."

I shuddered. Cold hot dogs were not my idea of a culinary delight. "Seven will be plenty. I only want one. Especially if we're having marshmallows for dessert."

I could almost taste the blackened cream puffs. It was a good thing I made it a habit never to diet during the holidays or on trips. Now I had a double reason to eat whatever I wanted. "I'll bring them out when you get the fire going."

"I appreciate you being a good sport." Phillip ran the back of his hand gently across my cheek as if to wipe away an imaginary tear.

A good sport? Is that what you call someone who has to be dragged kicking and screaming on a family trip? Oh, yeah, I should get an award. "No problem."

I knew he could tell I'd mentally rejected the compliment. But he just nodded and walked out to join the kids.

With inexperienced help, it would surely take Phillip half an hour to get the fire going. I grabbed the cell phone and punched in Vicky's number.

"Hello?"

"Hi, Vic. How's everything going there?"

"Penny? Where are you?"

"Through the looking glass?"

"That bad, huh?"

"No. . ." I thought of Donita and her kids having a home for Christmas. "Parts of it aren't bad at all."

"Spill."

"I'd rather hear about what's going on there."

"Well, Patty hosted the book group Christmas thing since you were gone. We laughed so hard, her husband stuck his head in to check on us." She squealed. *"Oh!* Guess what I got from my Secret Santa?"

"A book?" I guessed dryly.

"No! A basket with a mug and some cappuccino mix and a rolled-up fleece blanket. When I pulled the blanket out, there were three Ted Dekker books rolled up in it."

She'd gotten all that extra stuff and three books by my favorite author? And I got to spend the night at a burial site? Where was the fairness in that?

"That's great."

"Are you okay?"

Thankfully, Seth stuck his head in the door before I had to respond. "Mom! Where are the hot dogs?"

"I'm bringing them," I answered. "Vicky, I've got to go. Kiss the kids for me. I'll call you soon."

"Okay. Penny?"

"Yeah."

"I hope you have the best Christmas ever."

"You, too. I'll miss you." I pushed the END button and forced the tears from my eyes with a fake smile. The last thing our first family wiener roast needed was a weepy Willa. Besides I didn't even know what I was crying about. I was glad Vicky had fun at the party. I grabbed the hot dogs and ran out.

An hour later, we'd finished up with a marshmallow-eating contest, and even by the flickering light, I could see that Seth (the champion) had gotten it all over his face. I opened my mouth to tell him to run in and wash it off when Phillip stood.

"I thought we might spend some time with God tonight. . .as a family." Even though he wasn't talking loudly, his voice boomed in the near-deserted campground. "I mean. . ." He cleared his throat. "He's always with us, but He has given us so much, and sometimes I think, in our hurry to get along in the world, we forget to give our time and attention back to Him."

Amanda squirmed beside me. When Phillip produced his Bible from his jacket pocket, she looked at me with a furrowed brow.

I shrugged. Admittedly, Phillip had never talked much about God outside of the church building, but it wasn't that weird. Maybe the open fire reminded him of attending church camp when he was growing up.

Phillip read several verses from Colossians chapter 3 about putting on mercy and kindness and forgiving each other. Then he ended with verses 16 and 17.

" 'Let the word of Christ dwell in you richly in all wisdom; teaching and admonishing one another in psalms and hymns and spiritual songs, singing with grace in your hearts to the Lord. And whatsoever ye do in word or deed, do all in the name of the Lord Jesus, giving thanks to God and the Father by him.' " He put his Bible back into his pocket.

I was so glad he stopped there that I almost said, "Amen." I remembered the next verse of that chapter clearly from the ladies' class I'd just taught on submission. *"Wives, submit yourselves unto your own husbands, as it is fit in the Lord."*

Technically, I *had* submitted because I was here at the Meriwether Lewis Burial Site spending the night in an RV instead of at home hosting a party. But had my resentment been keeping me from doing it in a way *fit in the Lord?*

The next evening, Phillip guided the RV into a Wal-Mart parking lot.

"Oh, cool," Amanda said. "Are we going shopping?"

"Yes," Phillip answered. "We can go right now or we can go in the morning."

"Hmm. . ." I wrinkled my forehead. "Wouldn't it be better to just go now since we're here? So we won't have to drive back in the morning?"

Phillip swiveled around to face us. "That's the beauty of it. We're spending the night here tonight."

"You're kidding!" Seth looked out the window again as if to be sure we really were at Wal-Mart.

"Nope. I'm totally serious. I called ahead and asked permission for us to camp here tonight."

I had to choke down an incredulous laugh. "In the Wal-Mart parking lot?" He'd completely lost his mind.

He nodded.

Amanda switched back to the important part of what her dad had said earlier. "But we *are* going shopping?"

"You want to go now?"

She nodded. "There's this new CD. . ."

"I need some batteries," Seth added.

So that's why the handheld game had been *persona non grata* the last leg of the trip. What I'd thought was progress had actually been the untimely death of the Energizer bunny.

"We'll get a few camping supplies, but we're not really shopping for ourselves."

"Oh?" It was my turn to arch a brow. "Who are we shopping for?"

"Well, it's a—"

"—surprise!" Amanda and I finished together.

"How will we know what to buy?" she asked.

That mysterious black notebook appeared in his hands. He pulled out two pieces of paper. "Seth, you're with me. Amanda and Penny, here's yours." He passed one of the sheets to Amanda.

I fought the urge to snatch it from her as my curiosity burgeoned. Instead I looked over her shoulder at the strange list in Phillip's neat handwriting.

40 each of the following items:

Hairbrush with soft bristles
Hand lotion
Talcum powder
White tube socks
Box of stationery
Wall calendar with large numbers
Christmas cards

I gaped at our list. Had Phillip finally flipped his lid? Just as I leaned over to peek at the paper he and Seth were studying, he tucked it in his pocket and grinned.

Amanda and I obviously had more shopping experience than the guys, because we beat them back to the RV with everything on our list.

We laughed about getting there first as we carried the bags in and set them on the dinette table.

"Has Dad gone off the deep end or what?" Amanda asked.

So she'd finally figured out I wasn't to blame. Where was the comfort I should have taken in that?

"He just wants us to spend some time together." I grabbed a soda from the fridge and passed her one.

"Yeah, but right here at Christmas? And in an RV?" She popped the top on the can. "Most people would just institute a family game night."

I snorted cola out my nose. Her dry wit and big vocabulary never ceased to amaze me. Unfortunately I didn't get nearly enough chances to talk to her.

"Your dad's not 'most people.'"

"Is this the part where you tell me that we're on this trip because of some deficiency in his raising?"

I grinned. "I have no idea why we're on this trip."

"But you came anyway."

"It's really important to him." Who was the martyr now?

"So if you care about someone and they want you

184

to do something really important to them, even if you don't want to, you should do it?"

I sat my can on the table, hoping she didn't see my hand tremble. Was this conversation really going where I thought it was? As far as I knew, she didn't even like a particular boy. But no mama in her right mind would brush off a question like that.

"No, that's not necessarily true at all." I weighed every word like my life depended on it. If I ventured too close to her hidden meaning, she'd think I was lecturing and tune me out. *Lord, please give me the words.*

I suddenly remembered Tammy. I hadn't thought of her in years.

"In junior high, my friend Tammy wanted us to become blood sisters."

"Eww! Gross."

"Yeah, well, other kids did it. So, one night when I stayed at her house, she pulled out a knife and insisted that we prick our hands and smear them together."

Amanda shuddered. "You didn't do it, did you?"

"No, even though she was furious at me, I wouldn't go through with it. I loved her, but I knew it was wrong."

"Duh! Mom, you could have gotten AIDS! Or some other disease." The horror on her face made me know she'd remember Tammy for a long time to come.

Before I could respond, the door to the RV burst open, and we both jumped. The top of a small Scotch pine came sliding in the door, followed by the trunk and two proud Lassiter men.

The three-foot pine looked like the White House Christmas tree in the RV. We were afraid to put ornaments on it since we were pulling out the next morning. (Phillip had volunteered that top-secret information, believe it or not.) But we wrapped it in multicolored lights, and I think all of us watched it twinkle with some satisfaction. It was beginning to look a lot like Christmas.

That night after we were all tucked in bed, I lay in the dark, thinking of Phillip's thoughtful gesture. The tree, though small, had made great strides in breaking through my defenses. I padded over to get a drink, and by the parking lot light filtering in the window, I could see Seth snoring lightly in the overhead bunk. I turned automatically to check on Amanda.

The sofa was empty. I tiptoed back to the bathroom but she wasn't there. Sick fear clutched my stomach. There weren't that many places to hide in an RV.

I ran to the front door. It was unlocked. "Please, God. . . ," I murmured.

As soon as I opened the door I saw her. Clearly illuminated by the guard lights, she had her back to me, and she was talking on the cell phone. "Em, I know you gave me the money for a bus ticket, but I just can't do it. The 'rents would go bananas."

I stood with the door barely open. She was right. This half of the 'rents (short for "parents" in her language) was about to "go bananas." Suddenly our afternoon conversation took on a whole new meaning.

"You *are* my best friend," Amanda practically wailed. She was apparently too upset to worry about keeping her voice down. "And I don't want to miss your birthday party, but I have to."

I didn't know whether to grab the phone from her and throw it as far as I could or step back inside and let her handle things herself. She seemed to be doing a good job. Her next words made the whole world stop.

"I did plan to slip out tonight and catch a bus there, I promise. But I just can't. You have to understand." She sobbed hysterically.

Suddenly I knew what to do. I flung the door open, and in my reindeer flannel pajamas and Rudolph house shoes, I walked out into the Wal-Mart parking lot and touched Amanda's shoulder.

She gasped. "Em, I've got to go. I'm sorry." She ended the call and looked at my face, clearly searching for a clue to how I was feeling.

Good luck, girl. I had so many emotions right then *I* couldn't even sort them out.

She collapsed into my arms. The cold wind sluiced through us, but neither one of us cared. I held her until her sobs subsided.

"Are you okay?"

She nodded. "Am I grounded?"

I motioned toward the RV. "From what?"

"Oh, yeah." She sniffed. "Good point."

Chapter 8

. . .Eight Ladies Knitting

I woke Phillip when I went to bed and told him about the close call with Amanda. But I made him promise not to make a big deal out of it, and he agreed. She'd used her head. But what if she hadn't?

I shuddered again. Phillip pulled me against him and held me close until the sun peeped through the tiny bedroom window.

The next morning, while I fixed coffee, a subdued Amanda shot her daddy a nervous look with her good morning hug.

"I'm proud of you," I heard him say softly.

I was proud of him. A few weeks ago, he would

have ranted and raved about Emily being a bad influence. Maybe we were all learning.

After breakfast, we left Wal-Mart and changed direction. We drove about an hour before we pulled into the far corner of a small nursing home in northwest Tennessee, near the Kentucky line.

"I thought we'd bring the residents a little bit of early Christmas cheer," Phillip said. The mystery of the Wal-Mart lists was solved.

The kids looked like they wanted to refuse to go in, but one look at Phillip's face and I think they knew better.

Thirty minutes later, after we'd given out the gifts, Phillip and Seth went to hang a calendar in each resident's room.

Amanda and I were waiting in the lobby, shooting each other nervous looks, when a group of women streamed into the room.

One of the last ladies to enter grabbed Amanda's hands. "You've got the perfect hands for knitting, sweetie. It's time for our group. Come on and join us."

"Oh. No, thank you," Amanda said and gently extracted her hands from the woman's grasp, her face bright red.

The woman grabbed my hands and quickly dropped them. "Not as good, but maybe they'll do. You'll both come." She took my upper arm in one hand and Amanda's in the other. With surprising strength, she guided us to the couch.

I looked at Amanda and shrugged as the woman sank down between us.

"Essie Mae, help these girls get set up."

I wasn't entirely clear which woman was Essie Mae because they all handed us knitting needles and thread. Maybe she was the one with the red bandanna. . . .

"Mom!" I jerked my attention back to Amanda. She was glaring at me. "If you don't concentrate, we'll never learn."

I nodded.

Within seconds, the sound of knitting needles *click-clacked* in the air. The ladies had split up, and four of them were showing Amanda how to knit while the other four attempted to instruct me.

After twenty minutes of laughing at my own mistakes, I realized the woman had been right. My hands just weren't made for knitting. Amanda had caught on way better than I had. If *her* husband ever lost his job, their kids would have handmade hats, gloves, and scarves for Christmas. I bit back another laugh. Mine would just have to make do with apples and oranges.

"I'm sorry," I said. "I just can't do this."

The *click-clacking* stopped. In the eerie stillness, as eight (nine, if I counted Amanda) pairs of eyes stared at me in dismay, I shrugged. "I think my fingers are too big."

"Maybe if you could stop laughing and be serious...," Amanda scolded from her spot on the couch beside me. I think she'd decided that the sooner we learned to knit, the sooner we could escape.

As soon as she said that, I giggled. I couldn't help it. "Maybe I'm just overwhelmed by being in the presence of so much talent. Thank you so much for sharing with us." I passed the knitting needles and yarn to the woman next to me and stood. "We have to find my husband."

Amanda followed my lead. The women smiled and started knitting again.

"Smooth," Amanda whispered as we hurried away.

"Wonder where your dad and Seth got off to?" I asked.

Amanda looped her arm in mine. "You think a bunch of old men kidnapped them and are forcing them to learn how to do woodworking?"

I laughed. "That's a distinct possibility."

Just then they came into the lobby.

Seth ran up to us. "We hung calendars in forty rooms."

"Hmm. . .and all I did was learn to knit," Amanda quipped with a wry grin.

When we were back in the RV, Seth cleared his throat. "The place smelled kind of funny, but the whole nursing home thing wasn't half bad, you know it?"

Amanda nodded. "Kind of like you."

"Huh?"

She reached over and mussed his hair. "You're not half bad either once we get past your funny smell."

She started running before the words were completely out of her mouth, but by the time she got out the door, her little brother was less than a foot behind her.

"I really think she teases him because she loves him," I offered.

Phillip grinned. "Dream on."

Just a few miles from Kentucky, Phillip turned down the road leading to the Between the Lakes National Recreation Area. I gaped at the campground, which was almost completely surrounded by a sparkling lake, and for just an instant, I admitted to a tiny element of fun in this whole surprise thing.

Seth and Amanda bounced in their seats. Phillip grinned, looking much younger than he had just a week ago. The worry lines, ever-present in his face—especially during the last few months before he lost his job, had vanished. His blue eyes sparkled constantly now. And I was starting to think it was due to happiness instead of insanity.

After we had the motor home set, Phillip raised an eyebrow. "Who wants to go for a ride?"

"Me!" Seth was already halfway to the car.

"Me, too!" Amanda seconded as she took off like a shot after her brother.

Phillip studied my face. "You going?"

I looked at the sparkling water and the blue sky. God had plunked a brilliant spring day smack dab in the middle of December. And we were in one of the most beautiful places I'd ever seen. "You just try and keep me from it." I ran back in and grabbed my candy cane sweater.

By late afternoon, we'd hiked several trails and driven the length of The Trace, the road that ran between the lakes. Phillip joked that Amanda and I had taken so many pictures of the bison and elk that someday our great-grandkids would think they were their ancestors.

We were soaking in the last bit of daylight while puttering back to the campground when Amanda gasped.

"Daddy!" she yelled. "Stop the car."

Phillip mashed the brake. "What is it?"

She pointed to a tree a few yards off the road. A huge bird perched on a branch.

"A bald eagle," I breathed.

We fixed our gazes on him while I slowly rolled my window down. I snapped several pictures, but the majestic bird sat as still as a statue.

"Let's wait a few minutes," Seth whispered.

Phillip nodded. Just then, the eagle spread its wings and, with princely grace, soared into the sky. My heart ached at the beauty and splendor of his flight.

When the eagle had faded to a tiny speck and blended completely with the horizon, I rolled my window up and we rode back to the campground in silence.

That night around the campfire, it didn't seem odd when Phillip pulled out his Bible.

"I'm going to read tonight from the book of Isaiah, chapter forty, verse thirty-one." The fire crackled in the still night.

" 'But they that wait upon the Lord shall renew their strength; they shall mount up with wings as eagles.' " Just as it had the other night, Phillip's voice rang out. In my mind's eye, I could see the eagle soaring in the sky, so free, so powerful.

" 'They shall run, and not be weary; and they shall walk, and not faint.' "

The familiar verse gave me goose bumps. Patience had never been my strong suit. But I longed with every fiber of my being to soar, unfettered, like the eagle we'd seen that afternoon. Was this road trip part of my learning to wait on the Lord?

After we doused the fire, we sat at the picnic table in the dark and listened to the waves lapping against the shore.

"This is cool," Amanda murmured.

"Yeah, it is," Seth said. I couldn't see their faces very well, but they sounded as contented as I felt.

When the kids went in to get ready for bed, Phillip pulled me to my feet in the moonlight. He held me close and I listened to his heartbeat, not for reassurance that he wasn't an alien, but because I wondered if it, like Phillip himself, had grown stronger.

He tilted my chin to meet his gaze, and I didn't resist. "Forgive me?" he asked softly.

A big part of me wanted to say yes and melt into his arms. Another part wanted to stay irritated or even deny ever being mad in the first place. Plus, I'd realized moments before that Amanda and I had missed the mother/daughter shopping trip already. My emotions spun like a tilt-a-whirl.

The night was made for melting. I settled for standing on my tiptoes and pressing my lips to his and hoped he wouldn't notice I didn't answer.

He pulled away gently and dropped a tender kiss on my forehead. "I really do love you, Penny."

Before I could form a reply around the lump in my throat, he'd slipped into the RV. I put my fingers to my lips. *I think he noticed.*

Chapter 9

...Nine Candles Burning

A few miles past Mayfield, Kentucky, Phillip maneuvered the RV into a narrow driveway. Cars and trucks sat willy-nilly in the grassy lot, but the giant oak trees interlocked above the white church house with almost perfect symmetry. Even with no leaves the branches seemed to hold the little structure in a safe embrace.

I snuck a peek at the kitchen clock. We'd made it with five minutes to spare. I always feel like being late on Sunday morning is sort of like being sick. I never want to do it even if I'm at home, but it's something to be avoided at all costs when I'm visiting.

"Wow, it looks like something out of *Little House*

on the Prairie," Amanda whispered as we walked up on the porch.

It must have been TV Land day because when we walked in the door, the two elderly ladies who greeted us bore a striking resemblance to the Baldwin sisters from *The Waltons.*

Their suits were identical, one blue, the other lilac. Before I could think much about that, though, they grabbed my husband.

"Phillip? Is that you?"

Phillip nodded and hugged them tightly. While the kids and I stared, the lady in the blue suit pinched Phillip's cheek. It wouldn't have surprised me a bit if she'd said, "My, how you've grown."

Instead she said, "And this is your lovely family?"

Phillip, who had the grace to look embarrassed that he hadn't forewarned us about this particular surprise, nodded. He introduced us to his great-aunts, Earlene and Marla Houston.

I smiled, but if I'd been wearing false teeth I would have swallowed them. I *had* to find that black notebook of Phillip's.

Before we could get further acquainted, it was time for us to take our seats. I did note with pleasure that Aunt Earlene, who sat on the pew next to Phillip, pinched his cheek again and patted his knee several times.

After we were dismissed, both ladies turned to us. "Are y'all ready to go?"

Go?

"Yes, ma'am," Phillip said and cast me a wary glance.

I smiled brightly and nodded. I'm sure it's a pride issue, but I've always hated for people to know that I'm unaware of my family's actions or intentions. Even my kids understand this. They know that if they make a bad grade on a test or get in trouble at school, it's much to their advantage to tell me themselves. Because if they wait and let Trevor's mom or Becky's aunt waylay me in the grocery store to fill my ears with tales of what my child has been up to, there'll be trouble with a capital *T*. Of course, the few times that had happened, I smiled serenely at the tell-you-for-your-own-good woman as if I'd known it for days. So, Phillip knew he was safe from my questions for a while.

But when we climbed into the RV with the door safely closed, I slammed my purse onto the counter and followed Phillip into our room and shut the door. "What were those women talking about?" I took my shoes off and jabbed them one at a time in the bottom of the closet.

As I yanked off my dress and pulled my green and red sweatshirt over my head, Phillip smiled. "Nice shirt. What a surprise that you're wearing it."

I couldn't believe it. All week, he'd been ignoring my constant parade of Christmas clothes. And now he had the nerve to subtly compare his low-down, secret-keeping scheme to keep me in the dark with my harmless game of bringing Christmas to his mind by dressing like Holly Holiday.

"Aargh." I slid into my jeans, and as I tied my tennis shoes, my hands were shaking. "Tell me what your aunts were talking about."

"Oh, the sisters?" he said, like he'd forgotten we'd even seen his great-aunts that morning. "I thought we'd stay with them for a few days and do some work around their place." He grabbed a flannel shirt from the small closet. "Aunt Marla has bad arthritis, and Aunt Earlene is going blind. But they've both got sense enough to know they need some help." He buttoned it slowly. "It's okay with you, isn't it?"

I glared at him. Why didn't he just order me to do it? That way, I could be mad at him and not have to feel guilty for saying no, that wasn't okay. I remembered his aunts, smiling lovingly at our family and both wearing suits that had been around at least thirty years. It was obvious they couldn't afford to hire someone to do the work. "It's fine. I just like to know."

He nodded. "Can you be ready to leave in about ten minutes? They're fixing lunch for us."

He started out the door.

"Phillip?"

"Yeah?"

"What kind of work?"

He shrugged. "Light housekeeping and some odds-and-ends jobs."

I rolled my eyes. "Don't you know there's no such thing as 'light' housekeeping?"

He bent his head and kissed me. "Don't worry. It'll be fun."

🔔

"Fun," I grumbled under my breath when we arrived at the aunts' house. The house resembled a small plantation manor and had undoubtedly been beautiful in its time. But now, in *our* time, shutters hung by a thread and paint had peeled in too many places to count.

When we walked inside, the wonderful aroma made it impossible to think about anything else. Fried chicken? Mashed potatoes and gravy? Homemade rolls? Hadn't these ladies ever heard of counting fat grams?

Thankfully, they hadn't. Ten minutes after the meal (while we were washing dishes, actually), the food-induced haze started to wear off, and I took a good look at the interior of the house. Piles of newspapers and magazines rested on every table. Dust, thick enough to plant a garden, layered most surfaces, and it was almost impossible to see out the windows. And that was just in the kitchen.

After the last dish was put away, Phillip pulled out his black notebook and retrieved some blank pages. He passed them to me with a pen.

"We need to make a to-do list."

I bit back a hysterical giggle. *A to-do list?* We needed to call a demolition company. But I'd already grown attached to Aunt Earlene and Aunt Marla. (Who wouldn't grow attached to ladies who could cook like that?) So I just nodded and poised the pen over the paper.

"Who will volunteer to be my helper while I hang the shutters?"

"I will." Seth's eyes gleamed with excitement. It had been days since I'd seen his electronic friend, even though I knew for a fact that he'd gotten new batteries at Wal-Mart.

"Okay, put Seth and me down for repairing the shutters, honey."

Phillip pushed his chair back and stood, apparently too carried away with his commander-in-chief role to sit. "We have to gather the newspapers and magazines and take them to the recycling center."

"Oh, my," Aunt Earlene gasped.

"Now, Earlie, we promised Phillip on the phone that if he helped us we'd do what he says. And you know we can't see to read those anyway." Marla patted her sister's blue-veined hand.

"I'll handle the reading material," I volunteered, touched by their cooperative spirit. I knew how hard it was to throw out a magazine you hadn't read. Besides, I planned to take the older ones to an antique shop and see if I could get the sisters some extra money.

"I'll help." Amanda smiled shyly at Aunt Marla. For the first time in her young life, my daughter had discovered that all chocolate pies didn't come from a box marked "instant." She would probably do anything to get another one.

Over the next half hour, we split up the rest of the jobs, and I figured we'd just booked ourselves through New Year's Day, at least. The aunts wanted to sign up for some chores, but we assured them if they would just cook, we'd all be happy.

We agreed to start on Monday, so that afternoon we explored the grounds of the house where Phillip's grandmother had grown up.

Eventually, our exploring turned into the first impromptu family game of tag we'd had since the kids were in preschool. After ten minutes, we'd warmed up to it.

"Tag! You're it!" Seth touched my shoulder, and I froze.

"Mom," he wailed. "We're not playing freeze tag. We're just playing regular tag."

I nodded and put my hand to my side. "I know that, Son."

"You can't rest. You're it!" He was indignant.

"Aw, come on, Seth. Give her a break." Phillip ran up to me. "She can't help it if she's out of shape."

I reached out as if I were going to lean on Phillip for support. Instead I tapped him lightly on the shoulder. "Tag. You're it," I called as I ran off.

For a little while I was an eagle, soaring free and never growing tired.

The next morning, I landed with a thud.

"I found a wheelbarrow." Phillip greeted me at the door of the RV when I finally stumbled out at 6:30.

"Good for you."

"You and Amanda can use it to haul the papers and magazines to the car."

"Thanks." I relaxed in his arms for a minute. "Good morning."

He kissed me, then whispered close to my ear. "Are you sore from playing tag?"

I arched an eyebrow. "Like I would admit it."

"I am, too." Phillip grinned. "But we'll work out the soreness today."

For the next three days, I waited to "work out the soreness," but instead it just seemed to multiply. By Thursday morning, though, I could see some difference in the house.

"How long do you plan to stay here?" I asked Phillip as I sipped my coffee. It was 7:00 a.m., but Seth and Amanda had been working so hard we'd decided to let them sleep in.

"Are you ready to leave?"

"No!" My face grew hot. "I. . .well, to be honest, I hate to leave until we finish."

"Me, too. I was thinking we could be ready to paint by the weekend. Then if we paint Saturday, take Sunday off. . ." He smiled, and I knew we were both remembering the meal we'd enjoyed last Sunday.

Though the aunts prepared mouthwatering meals every day, none had been as decadently delicious as that first one. He cleared his throat and took a big sip of coffee. ". . .and paint Monday and Tuesday, we'll be done."

"Three days to paint the whole house?"

"If the four of us work together. Plus, a few people from the church said they'd come help us Saturday."

He shrugged. "We might have to come back this summer and do the second coat. Would you mind?"

"You're asking me about a trip in advance?" The challenge slipped out before I thought.

He turned beet red. "If I'd asked you about this one, what would you have said?"

Before I could answer, the cell phone rang. Phillip looked at the caller ID and frowned. "It's your folks."

I frowned, too, as I reached for it. My mom believed cell phones should only be used in life-and-death circumstances.

"Hello?"

"Penny? Is that you?"

"Hey, Mom. It's me. What's wrong?"

"The presents didn't come."

"What?"

"You told me to call you if the presents you sent didn't come. So I'm calling. We didn't get them."

"Oh, no."

"We don't care one bit about that, Penny. And you know it. But you asked me to call you."

"Okay, Mom. Thanks for calling."

"We'll miss you, honey. Give Phillip and the children our love."

"We love all of y'all, too."

I pushed the END button and stared at the phone.

I had a sudden desire to fling it across the room.

Phillip was still frowning. "Penny, what happened? Are your parents okay?"

I nodded. "Remember the presents you mailed that Saturday before we left? They still haven't gotten them."

He just shook his head in what I could only assume was silent sympathy, then got up and headed out the door to work.

That afternoon, Amanda had gone out to take a break, and I was sitting in the den going through the piles of magazines. Not long after we'd started, I'd found the deed to the house between a 1940 *Collier's Weekly* and a 1946 *Saturday Evening Post*. So they all had to be sorted through individually.

I picked up a *Good Housekeeping* magazine from the early '80s, and a stack of photos slid out. When I reached to retrieve them, a small plastic bag with birthday candles in it tumbled to the floor on top of them. I grabbed the bag and dropped it in the shoe box I'd labeled *Keepsakes*, then gathered the photos. Before I could put them in the box for pictures, a familiar face caught my eye.

I held the grainy color snapshot closer to my eyes.

A small boy stood between Aunt Marla and Aunt Earlene. It looked just like Phillip, but they were clearly standing in front of this house. He would have mentioned being here before, wouldn't he?

I flipped through the rest of the pictures. The same little boy playing in a sprinkler on the lawn, then eating a slice of watermelon, and next, proudly displaying a green snake. The last picture was a close-up of him blowing out birthday candles. Inscribed in red icing on the cake were the words *Happy 9th Birthday, Phillip.* I glanced at the candles in the Ziploc bag and jumped to my feet, pictures still in my hand.

"Um. . .Aunt Marla. . ."

"Yes, dear?" She hobbled from the kitchen, wiping her hands on the cloth she wore fastened on her apron.

"Did Phillip visit y'all when he was a child?"

She nodded. "What a lovely summer that was. Earlene and I haven't felt that young since." A shadow passed over her face. "Too bad it couldn't have come under better circumstances."

"What do you mean?"

"Well, you know. When Richard left so suddenlike, poor Janet just couldn't handle Phillip. . . ." Her voice trailed off and her eyes grew cloudy.

Phillip's dad had left? What was she talking about?

Chapter 10

...Ten Painters Painting

I cleared my throat.

Aunt Marla jumped slightly. "Where was I? Oh, yes, Janet just couldn't handle little Phillip for a while. So she sent him to stay with us until she got on her feet."

"Oh, I see." *Said the blind woman.* "So he stayed all summer?"

"Uh-huh. By fall, Janet had gotten her nerves under control. She depended on him hard for the next several years, though, so he never did get to come back and see us."

Years? I felt dizzy. She must be mixed-up. Phillip had been twenty when we started dating, and I'd met his parents shortly after. They'd seemed perfectly happy. No one had ever mentioned otherwise.

"I need some air."

"I completely understand, honey. There's so much dust in those magazines."

I held up the pictures. "Is it okay if I take these with me for a while?" I strove to keep my tone casual.

"Oh, sure. Phillip might like to look at them."

"That's just what I was thinking." I walked out to the porch where Phillip worked alone. A quick glance showed Seth and Amanda sitting out by the RV.

"Phillip?"

He spun around and sawdust flew from his hair. "Hey. How's it going in there?"

"Pretty good." I glanced at the house. I had no idea how soundproof the walls were, and I didn't want to be overheard. "Want to go for a walk?"

He glanced at the sandpaper in his hand, then dropped it to the workbench. "Sure."

We walked off the porch and headed down a little lane that led to a long-neglected orchard on the back of the property. He cast me a sideways glance. "What's up?"

"I guess I'm just wondering why you've been keeping secrets from me."

"Oh, come on, Penny." He picked up a dead stick and threw it. "This has just been a game. You and I have both known that anytime you got really ready to know where we were going, I'd have told you. I offered to before we even left."

"So when were you going to tell me about this?" I thrust the pictures at him like a wife confronting her husband with proof of his infidelity.

He took the photos from my hand and stared at them. Red crept up his cheeks. "I spent the summer here the year I turned nine," he mumbled.

"We drove in here Sunday, and you acted for all the world like you'd never been here before. Why didn't you tell me?"

Phillip sank to the ground and pulled his knees up to his chest. "I just couldn't."

Oh, God, if this is a good time for You, I could really use that new heart right now, because this old selfish one wants to ask him a million questions and demand some answers.

The new carefree Phillip had gone just as quickly as he'd come. As he stared across the desolate orchard, the worry lines creased his face. At the sight of his slumped shoulders, all the anger and resentment of the last few weeks fell away, leaving my soul as bare as the tree branches.

I knelt down beside him and touched his shoulder. "Honey, I'm sorry I've been so awful."

He looked at me like he'd forgotten I was there. Then he shook his head. "You haven't."

I snorted. "Yes, I have, and you know it."

A hint of a grin teased across his face. "Well, okay, maybe a little, but I have, too."

We sat quietly in the dry grass, shoulders touching.

"When I was eight, my dad left. No explanations. He just told my mom he was leaving and he left." He fiddled with a piece of grass and didn't look at me. "Mom sent me here for the summer. I guess she just couldn't take my questions about Dad."

"That must have been tough for you."

He looked up then. "In some ways it was awful. I missed Mom so much, not to mention Dad. But the aunts smothered me with love, and at least here, nobody was crying all the time."

I remembered Aunt Marla's words. "And in the fall, you went home and worked to help your mom."

He nodded. "Then one day when I was sixteen, Dad showed up on our doorstep. He apologized and begged us to take him back. Mom was so happy that I didn't have the heart to stay mad at him."

"That was a lot for a teenager to deal with." I thought of Amanda and her fluctuating emotions.

"It was tough for a while. We moved to another town so we could start over without anyone knowing.

We made sort of a silent vow to each other to act like those years had never happened."

I could see why he'd kept it a secret, but how could I have not known that for sixteen years he'd been holding part of himself back?

"I wanted to tell you, Pen. I really did. But I knew my parents desperately wanted to forget it."

"I understand." To my amazement, I really did. Had God moved me to the top of His heart transplant list?

Six days later, we hugged the aunts and promised to come back next summer to put a second coat of paint on the house. As we pulled out of the driveway, I peeked through the window once more to admire our handiwork. The old house looked like a mansion.

A family from church had helped us paint Saturday, and with the ten of us working, we'd covered a huge amount of ground. . .um. . .board.

The husband and wife were a sweet couple with twin sons Seth's age and a daughter Amanda's age, and we'd all gotten along famously. But the whipped topping on the homemade chocolate pie—in Amanda's eyes anyway—had been their shy, but cute, sixteen-year-old son.

I knew for a fact that he and Amanda had exchanged

e-mail addresses. And not because I'd overheard it either, but because she'd told me.

Two days later, we were rolling merrily across southern Missouri, headed who knew where. Well, Phillip knew, of course, but the rest of us didn't. I was partly watching the scenery fly by, partly dozing. Amanda had developed a sudden interest in Christian romance, so she was reading one of my new Heartsongs. (I had to remind her daddy that she'd be fifteen in two weeks. He'd just cringed.)

"Stop, Dad!" Seth yelled from his post by the window.

I peered out as Phillip obligingly pulled into a circle driveway. I didn't see any wildlife.

"What is it?" Phillip turned to Seth when we were stopped.

"There was a really old man two houses back trying to put up his Christmas lights. I could see him from pretty far off, and he was having a hard time."

Phillip frowned. "And?"

"And we need to go help him."

"Go help him?" Phillip asked. "We don't even know him."

I saw the hurt expression on Seth's face fast enough

to swallow my own skeptical response.

"That sounds like a great idea, Seth." I raised an eyebrow at Phillip. "Do good deeds have to be prerecorded in your notebook? Or are we allowed to just do them randomly?"

He gave me a look that said, "You know we can't just go up to a stranger and offer to help with his Christmas lights." And I gave him one right back that said, "That's not any crazier than some of the things you've done."

Seth and Amanda watched the silent interchange between us with apparent interest.

Finally Phillip shrugged. "Okay, but you're going to do the talking, Seth."

Seth nodded and Phillip looped around the circle drive and eased back on the road.

The man was definitely a senior citizen, and from the looks of it, Seth had sized up the situation exactly. We pulled into his driveway, thankfully, another circle.

Phillip had barely stopped when Seth jumped out and ran over to the startled man. We couldn't hear him, but we could see his mouth moving rapidly, and then the man grinned and nodded.

Seth motioned us to come on.

"I don't believe this," Amanda grumbled as we

piled out of the RV.

"This is Mr. Reynolds," Seth announced as proudly as a first grader with a big frog for show-and-tell.

Phillip shook hands with the man and introduced Amanda and me.

"So you folks are on a good-deed trip, huh?" Mr. Reynolds's eyes were a little clouded, but a twinkle still lurked in the depths.

I watched the red creep up Phillip's face.

"Yes, sir," he replied. "Something like that."

"Well, bless my bones. I sure wouldn't want to deprive you from doing a good turn, so if you'd help me get these lights up, I'd be mighty obliged."

"We'd be glad to." Phillip took the string of lights from the old man and climbed the ladder. Seth grabbed the stapler and passed it up to his dad.

"Won't my wife be surprised when I go get her after awhile?" Mr. Reynolds's smile covered his whole face. "She's been in the hospital with the flu, but she's coming home today."

"I'm so glad she's able to come home," I said. And I was so glad that Seth had made us stop.

"Me, too. Me, too. But I'm tempted to call and see if they'll keep her until this evenin' so she can see the lights a-twinkling when we pull into the driveway."

"I. . ." I had no idea what to say to that.

Mr. Reynolds didn't seem to mind my loss for words. He moved closer to where Phillip and Seth were working.

I glanced at Amanda and she raised both eyebrows. "Was he serious?" she mouthed.

I shrugged. I could see the weird logic in waiting until evening. But I doubted Medicare or his wife would agree.

Twenty minutes later, after we'd tested all the lights, Mr. Reynolds shook our hands and thanked us. "I'm going to run on and pick the missus up from the hospital." He winked at Amanda. "I don't think she'd take too kindly to being left there all day for no reason." He smiled. "Y'all have a safe trip."

Amanda and I barely made it inside the RV before we collapsed into giggles.

"Women," Seth said in a disgusted tone.

"Yep." Phillip pulled onto the highway with a grin.

Chapter 11

. . .Eleven Roses Blooming

Late one night about a week before Christmas, we pulled into a campground in Springfield, Missouri. Both kids had zonked out hours before.

Phillip looked over at me. "You asleep?"

I shook my head. "Nope. Just thinking." *Wondering what your past has to do with our trip.* I bit my tongue.

He motioned toward the kids. "Think they'll be excited when they wake up in the morning and realize where we are?"

"I'd say that's an understatement." They'd driven Phillip crazy since we crossed the Missouri state line, begging to visit their cousins.

"I guess we'll see your cousin and his family at church tomorrow?"

Phillip leaned across the console. "What would you be willing to exchange for that information?"

"Hmm. . ." I leaned toward him. "Guess you'll just have to tell me and find out."

"Yes, we'll see them in the morning," he whispered against my lips, and I kissed him soundly.

I started to climb back to get the kids settled in bed, but he grabbed my arm. I swung around and he waved his black notebook in front of my nose. "What's this worth to you?"

I giggled softly. "Actually, you can keep it. I think I'm starting to enjoy being surprised."

I remembered those words the following night when just the two of us drove back to the campground from his cousin's house.

"Three days?" I asked. "The kids are going to stay with them for three days?" I had to admit, I'd gotten used to us all being packed in together in the RV like gifts in a stocking.

"Unless you have a problem with it."

"Was this in your notebook?" Could he and the kids have cooked this up after we got here? Nobody had seemed surprised but me. And I'd hidden it well, of course.

He nodded. "I talked to John and Paula about it before we left home. Did you think I'd forgotten that our anniversary is tomorrow?"

"No, but I never dreamed you'd planned anything like this."

"Never underestimate your husband, Mrs. Lassiter."

"Believe me, I'm learning not to."

When I opened my eyes the next morning, a red rose rested on my pillow a few inches away from my nose. *Whoa.* Had a stranger abducted Phillip in the middle of the night and replaced him with a Stepford husband? Phillip was nothing if not pragmatic, and he would never put a rose on my pillow, in case I rolled over and stuck myself on the thorns.

I squinted at the stem and burst out laughing. It had been carefully de-thorned. Now that was something Phillip would do.

Now that I was awake, I smelled coffee. "Phillip?"

He stepped to the bedroom door. "Good morning. I thought you were going to sleep all day."

"Happy Anniversary," I said with a smile. "I won." We have a standing game to see which one can tell the other one happy anniversary or Valentine's Day or even Thanksgiving Day first. He'd had the perfect chance to win, but he'd blown it with "Good morning."

"Afraid not. That rose was my 'happy anniversary' to you."

I rolled back over, and sure enough, a little tag on the stem proclaimed "Happy Anniversary." I scrunched up my nose. "Cheater. But thanks for the rose."

"There are eleven more to go with it." He nodded toward the nightstand where an elegant bouquet of a dozen roses, minus one de-thorned one, soaked in a crystal vase full of water.

Two days ago, I'd been imagining what it would be like to have our anniversary on this trip. My musings couldn't have been further from reality. "They're beautiful." I stretched and yawned. "How did you get those so early?"

"I got up at the crack of dawn. Unlike somebody I know." He grinned and leaned against the doorframe.

I sat up in bed and stretched again. It had been wonderful to sleep late. All the way across Missouri, Phillip had found volunteer opportunities for us, from caroling in the campground to raking leaves at a senior citizens' center. We teased him about not wanting to make Seth out to be a liar about our "good-deed tour."

"So what do we have planned today?"

"What do you want to do?"

"So suddenly you've lost your notebook?" I grinned to take the sting out of my words.

"No, I've got it all planned, but I thought you might be getting a little sick of that."

"If it doesn't involve volunteering somewhere, I'd just as soon follow your plan."

"In that case, pack enough clothes for two days and two nights."

"Um. . .pack? In case you haven't noticed, we're living in our room already."

He bent down and kissed me. "Are you going to go along with the plan, or are you going to complain all day?"

"I don't know," I teased. "Was that kiss my punishment for complaining or incentive to comply?"

"Incentive."

"Then I'm definitely packing."

He grinned and kissed me again. "I'm going to go up to the office and let them know we'll be gone a couple of days."

I watched him leave, then packed enough for both of us for two days. I included one nice outfit each, just in case. I was getting pretty good at "just in case."

With the suitcases ready, I carried the bouquet of eleven roses into the kitchen and set them on the table. I'd wrapped the single, de-thorned bloom in tissue and stashed it in my bag. Nothing said romance like a single rose on your pillow, and tonight *was* our anniversary night.

Finally, I sat down for a cup of coffee and rubbed a soft rose petal between my fingers. Had he bought me roses because he really loved me? Or because it was what he thought I expected? For the first time I could remember, his motivation was more important to me than his actions.

For our whole married life, I'd treated Phillip like he was an extension of me. We'd had disagreements, and I knew he was the "head" of our household; but I had just never thought that much about his feelings, except in direct relation to my own.

The strength and the vulnerability I'd seen in him these past few weeks had changed my love. Deepened it. And my inner struggle to submit to him willingly, out of love and not out of duty, had made a difference, as well.

He opened the door just as I was dabbing my tears. "Penny? Are you crying?"

"No." *Not in the last two seconds.*

He sank across from me and took my hand. "Has this trip been so awful?"

I shook my head. "It's been fun, really." And it had. We'd all laughed more together in the last month than we had in the last year.

"But you still wonder why I insisted we do it." He got up and poured himself a cup of coffee.

I chuckled. "Well, now that you mention it. . ."

"You probably know it has something to do with my dad."

"I thought it might."

"You don't miss a trick, do you?" he chided, but I recognized the teasing glint in his eyes.

"Hopefully not anymore. Not if it has to do with you." My early New Year's resolution was to pay way more attention in the future. If I hadn't been so wrapped up in myself, Phillip might have told me about his childhood much earlier.

"A couple of months ago, when Dad had his heart attack, remember I spent the night with him that first night?"

I nodded.

"We didn't know if he would make it through the night, and he wanted to talk. For the first time, after all these years, he told me why he left."

"Why?" Another woman, no doubt.

"He said he left because he'd spent so much of his time and energy making a living that the people in his house had become strangers to him, and as strangers, it was easy to walk away from them."

"Well, that seems a little oversimplified." I grabbed

my tongue between my teeth. *Be still, Penny, and listen.*

"Maybe so, but after he said that and warned me not to make the same mistake, I came home to a house where I felt like an intruder. I didn't feel like I knew you or the kids anymore, and when I tried to turn to God, I found I didn't know Him anymore either, and the realization scared me worse than any horror movie ever could."

I wanted to protest, but I just bit my tongue harder.

Phillip pulled me to my feet and folded me into his arms. "I've still got a long way to go. But I finally know God again—and you and the kids, too—and I'll never let y'all go as long as there is breath in my body. This crazy trip gave that back to me." He kissed me, and I knew he was right. Somehow, out on the open road, we'd all found our way home.

Chapter 12

. . . Twelve Gifts of Love

T was the night before Christmas and in the RV, the Lassiter family curled up by the tree. I took another sip of hot cocoa and surveyed the scene. I almost wished I were a cat so I could purr.

Wrapping paper littered the floor. Amanda sat on the love seat, writing in her new journal, and Seth sorted through the tool set Phillip had bought for him. He was already planning which tools to take to the aunts' house next summer.

Phillip and I had spent our anniversary in Branson, which was what he'd planned all along. It was the first anniversary in years when it hadn't really mattered *what* we did, as long as we were together. It was a good feeling.

After we'd picked up the kids, we went shopping. Working without a list had been a challenge, but I think we had all risen to it. We each bought one gift per family member, so we'd only had twelve gifts under the tree. But the tree was so small that it had looked just right. And it was.

Traditionally, we opened our gifts to each other on Christmas Eve, since we always spent Christmas Day with my parents. Although he hadn't spelled it out (and no, I didn't steal his black notebook—it was almost flat now), I'd surmised that Phillip had a big volunteer gig planned for Christmas Day, so we'd decided to continue our tradition.

Phillip stretched out beside me on the carpet and flipped the pages of the deluxe-version travel atlas I'd gotten him.

"Look, honey. Wouldn't you like to go there?" He pointed to an obscure part of Brazil.

Jungles? my inner child wailed. *What about spiders and snakes?*

I just smiled. "It looks. . .interesting, but it might be hard to do that on a two-week vacation. Maybe we should stick with the States for now."

"I guess you're right." He closed the book suddenly. "Penny, did you open the package from me?"

"No."

"Are you sure? It was small."

"I'm sure." The smallest thing I'd opened had been a new Ted Dekker book from Amanda.

He scrounged around under the wrapping paper and handed me a small square box.

Before I opened it, I looked again at Phillip, Seth, and Amanda all here with me, in body and in spirit. What more could a woman want? *"Girl,"* my inner child corrected me. *What more could a* "girl" *want?* I shook my head at her silliness and tore the box open.

Nestled on soft cotton, a crystal heart ornament shimmered in the light. Below the etching of a couple on a sleigh ride were the words *Our First Christmas Together.*

I couldn't believe it. I'd gotten my new heart.

"Wake up, sleepyhead," Phillip whispered in my ear. I jumped and slammed into my seat belt. Then I remembered. He'd had us sleep buckled in so he could drive through the night to wherever we were volunteering today.

My muscles ached from sleeping in the chair. How could I face a day of cutting up vegetables and handing out soup the way I felt? Heat flushed my face. If hungry people could face standing in line to get it, I could surely face standing in line to hand it out.

"I'm sore." Sometimes my inner child insisted on waking up before me so she could talk out loud.

"Here, let me rub your back." Phillip swiveled his chair toward me, and I leaned forward with my eyes still closed while he kneaded the tired muscles.

"I should be rubbing your back. Where did we have to be today that you had to drive all night to get us there?" I rubbed my bleary eyes and peered out the window.

"Phillip!" My parents' house was directly across the road from where we were parked. Tears streamed down my cheeks. "You didn't have to do this."

"I wanted to surprise you."

Suddenly I remembered Mom's phone call. "Uh-oh." I put my hand to my mouth. "We don't have any gifts." I looked at the familiar house and twisted back around to grin at my amazing husband. "Oh, well, so what? They'll have us. . .and we'll have them." It seemed odd that a year ago, I'd thought carrying in an armload of gaily wrapped packages and steaming covered dishes was the most important thing.

I hugged him again.

He cleared his throat. "But it just so happens we do have presents for them."

I arched a brow. "What do you mean?"

"Well, since this was my scheduled ending to our

trip, I didn't mail the packages. I was afraid they might open them before we got here, so I just brought them with us."

I squealed. "You're kidding!"

He shook his head. "They're in the storage underneath."

I couldn't sit still another second. I leaped past the console, my earlier soreness a distant memory.

"Seth! Amanda! Guess where we are!"

I tickled Amanda's bare foot.

"Huh? Mom. Don't." She snuggled farther into her pillow.

"You've got to get up, both of you!" I gave Phillip a pleading look. "Help me! You know my mom comes out to get her newspaper the first thing."

He laughed. "Calm down. They'll get up when they realize where we are."

Ten minutes later, while the kids—finally awake and excited—were dressing, I hurried out to help Phillip get the gifts from the storage. Just as we stepped outside, the front door of the house opened.

Mom stepped onto the porch in her duster and house shoes and scooped up the newspaper. When she straightened, her gaze fell on the RV. She stood frozen for a few seconds. Then, still clutching the paper, she raced toward us.

I ran to meet her and we fell into each other's arms, spinning together like schoolgirls. "Merry Christmas!" I cried.

"Penny! Y'all made it home!"

I looked over her shoulder at the love shining in Phillip's eyes and then to where Seth and Amanda were climbing out of the RV with sleepy smiles. "Yes, Mama, we sure did."

CHRISTINE LYNXWILER thanks God daily for the joyous life she shares with her husband and two daughters. They work, play, and worship together in a small Arkansas town nestled in the Ozark Mountains. Besides writing and spending time with her family, Christine enjoys reading, kayaking, trout fishing, and going to auctions. She loves to hear from her readers.

A Letter to Our Readers

Dear Readers:

In order that we might better contribute to your reading enjoyment, we would appreciate your taking a few minutes to respond to the following questions. When completed, please return to the following: Fiction Editor, Barbour Publishing, Inc., P.O. Box 719, Uhrichsville, OH 44683.

1. Did you enjoy reading *All Jingled Out*?
   ❑ Very much—I would like to see more books like this.
   ❑ Moderately—I would have enjoyed it more if _____
   _____
   _____

2. What influenced your decision to purchase this book?
   (Check those that apply.)
   ❑ Cover   ❑ Back cover copy   ❑ Title   ❑ Price
   ❑ Friends   ❑ Publicity   ❑ Other

3. Which story was your favorite?
   ❑ *All Done with the Dashing*   ❑ *My True Love Gave to Me*

4. Please check your age range:
   ❑ Under 18   ❑ 18–24   ❑ 25–34
   ❑ 35–45   ❑ 46–55   ❑ Over 55

5. How many hours per week do you read? _____

Name _____

Occupation _____

Address _____

City _____ State _____ Zip _____

E-mail _____

If you enjoyed

All Jingled Out

then read:

ROOM AT THE INN

*Love Checks Into Two
Christmas Novellas*

Orange Blossom Christmas by Kristy Dykes
Mustangs and Mistletoe by Pamela M. Griffin

If you enjoyed

All Jingled Out

then read:

A PRAIRIE CHRISTMAS

*A Pair of Novellas Celebrating
the Age-Old Season of Love*

One Wintry Night by Pamela M. Griffin
The Christmas Necklace by Maryn Langer

JHEARTSONG ❤ PRESENTS

Love Stories
Are Rated G!

That's for godly, gratifying, and of course, great! If you love a thrilling love story but don't appreciate the sordidness of some popular paperback romances, **Heartsong Presents** is for you. In fact, **Heartsong Presents** is the premiere inspirational romance book club featuring love stories where Christian faith is the primary ingredient in a marriage relationship.

Sign up today to receive your first set of four, never-before-published Christian romances. Send no money now; you will receive a bill with the first shipment. You may cancel at any time without obligation, and if you aren't completely satisfied with any selection, you may return the books for an immediate refund!

Imagine. . .four new romances every four weeks—two historical, two contemporary—with men and women like you who long to meet the one God has chosen as the love of their lives. . .all for the low price of $10.99 postpaid.

To join, simply complete the coupon below and mail to the address provided. **Heartsong Presents** romances are rated G for another reason: They'll arrive Godspeed!

YES! Sign me up for Heart❤ng!

NEW MEMBERSHIPS WILL BE SHIPPED IMMEDIATELY!
Send no money now. We'll bill you only $10.99 postpaid with your first shipment of four books. Or for faster action, call toll free 1-800-847-8270.

NAME _____

ADDRESS _____

CITY _____ STATE _____ ZIP _____

MAIL TO: HEARTSONG PRESENTS, P.O. Box 721, Uhrichsville, Ohio 44683
or visit www.heartsongpresents.com